"I've been waiting all day for you to come in alone."

Terror blindsided Kate. "What do you want?"

"You. Let's go."

A knock on the door made them both jerk and she sucked in a ragged breath.

"Kate?" Lucas's voice sounded from the other side. "I'm going to let your dog out. You okay?"

She stayed silent.

The gun jabbed once more. "Answer him."

"Kate?"

"Help!" She spun, praying the attacker wouldn't pull the trigger.

Rocky Mountain K-9 Unit

These police officers fight for justice with the help of their brave canine partners.

Lynette Eason is a bestselling, award-winning author who makes her home in South Carolina with her husband and two teenage children. She enjoys traveling, spending time with her family and teaching at various writing conferences around the country. She is a member of Romance Writers of America and American Christian Fiction Writers. Lynette can often be found online interacting with her readers. You can find her at Facebook.com/lynette.eason and on Twitter, @lynetteeason.

Books by Lynette Eason

Love Inspired Suspense

Rocky Mountain K-9 Unit

True Blue K-9 Unit

Wrangler's Corner

Visit the Author Profile page at LoveInspired.com for more titles.

RESCUE MISSION

LYNETTE EASON

LOVE INSPIRED SUSPENSE
INSPIRATIONAL ROMANCE

Special thanks and acknowledgment are given to Lynette Eason for her contribution to the Rocky Mountain K-9 Unit miniseries.

LOVE INSPIRED® SUSPENSE
INSPIRATIONAL ROMANCE

Recycling programs
for this product may
not exist in your area.

ISBN-13: 978-1-335-58804-3

Rescue Mission

Copyright © 2022 by Harlequin Enterprises ULC

For questions and comments about the quality of this book, please contact us at CustomerService@Harlequin.com.

Love Inspired
22 Adelaide St. West, 41st Floor
Toronto, Ontario M5H 4E3, Canada
www.LoveInspired.com

Printed in U.S.A.

Grace be to you and peace from God the Father, and from our Lord Jesus Christ, who gave himself for our sins, that he might deliver us from this present evil world.

—*Galatians* 1:3-4

Dedicated to those who put their lives on the line for others. Thank you for your service.

ONE

Kate Montgomery rolled over in the unfamiliar bed and punched the flat pillow. Had she ever felt so alone? Her first night in Montana was in a small rental in an obscure neighborhood not too far outside of Bozeman. Just one night and then she could go on to the cabin her friend had arranged for her to stay in. She'd run a long way from Denver, but apparently, she couldn't outrun the nightmares that plagued her.

Not even Cocoa's warm, furry presence could keep the images from returning every time she closed her eyes. She scratched the little mutt's silky ears and sighed. Skylar Morgan, a detective with the Denver Police Department, had recommended the tiny shaggy cocoa-colored pup and it had been one of the best ideas ever. Cocoa stretched then settled only to roll to her feet and bark. "Shh. Be quiet, Cocoa. Lie down."

But the dog stayed on her feet and Kate groaned. She was exhausted from her journey and needed to sleep. To continue to heal from the car accident that had left her in a coma for weeks.

The car accident that hadn't been an accident.

She buried her face in the pillow. At least it smelled clean and fresh. Cocoa barked again and paced the length of the mattress before climbing up to lick Kate's face.

"Cocoa, come on, sweetie. I'm going to have to put you in the crate if you don't behave."

The old battery-powered clock on the nightstand ticked softly, and her eyelids grew heavy once more. Kate let herself drift in spite of what she knew was coming.

Heat pressed in on her. Panic grabbed at her. She couldn't move and the flames licked closer, surrounding the vehicle, singeing her skin. A baby's cry sent urgency sweeping over her, and she grabbed at the handle.

Get out! Get out!

Kate's eyes flew open, and she gasped. Cocoa barked, three rapid short yaps. Kate flipped to her back, and sweat rolled down her temples. She used a sheet to wipe it away then curled her shaking hands into fists. Would she ever have another night of uninterrupted sleep? She reached for Cocoa, needing her close and to stop her barking, but, instead of the dog, her hand landed on a hard object. An arm.

Someone's *arm*?

A scream gathered in her throat, and she rolled just as a rough hand clamped over her mouth and nose, cutting off her air and pinning her to the bed. Her nightmare had morphed into terrifying reality.

She couldn't breathe!

She bucked and twisted, dislodging the fingers for a fraction of a second. Just enough to grab a lungful of air, but he was so strong she'd never be able to fight him off. Panic closed in. She flailed her hands, beat on the arm, desperate to escape him. The edge of her wrist slammed against the nightstand. Whimpers stuck in her throat, and her fingers curled around something…the letter opener she'd found on the desk and used to tighten the loose knob on the nightstand. She grabbed the opener and aimed it toward the arm attached to the hand over her face.

"Ah!" The attacker's yell echoed through her small room. He jerked back and she jabbed again, aiming for whatever she could hit. Her hit was true, and he cried out again, stumbling away from the bed. She jumped up and ran. Cocoa followed, yapping at her heels.

Kate made it to the front door, threw it open and raced out into the freezing night air. With a frantic glance over her shoulder, her bare feet pounded the frozen ground.

She slammed into a hard chest, and a scream ripped from her throat. Hard hands grasped for her and slipped over her chilled skin. She fell, landing on her right hip. Pain raced through her, and she let out a harsh gasp, stunned into stillness for a brief second. Cocoa jumped at her, pulling her out of her dazed moment. She gathered the little dog in her arms and scrambled to her feet, ignoring the throbbing ache in her hip. She had to get away. The thought materialized even as she registered a voice calling her name.

"Kate? Hey, Kate, are you okay? What's going on?"

She went still once again. She knew that voice but wasn't sure why. She blinked up at the man holding her. A guy with brown hair and crystal blue eyes stared down at her. She scrambled backward, forcing him to drop his hands. "Who are you?" she asked. "Why were you in my house?" A shiver racked her, and her feet were quickly turning into blocks of ice while her teeth chattered.

"I wasn't," he said, "but we need to get you somewhere warm."

He rested a hand on the head of the beautiful dog sitting at his side. Still, Kate backed farther away, her bare feet numb, making it difficult to walk. "Someone was."

"Wasn't me. I'm Lucas Hudson with the Rocky Mountain K-9 Unit, and this is Angel." He stroked the ears of the border collie. The dog seemed quite content to let him do so. "Skylar Morgan called me and asked me to come check on you," Lucas said. "Looks like it's a good thing I did. Now, can we get you warmed up before you catch pneumonia or get frostbite?"

Hearing her friend's name roll from his lips nearly sent her to her knees. That and the fact he was with the RMKU. She should have recognized the understated uniform. Khaki pants, navy blue shirt and the badge on a chain around her neck. "Oh, thank you." Another violent shudder rippled through her and this time she paid attention to how cold she was.

Apparently, Lucas did, too. "Come with me."

"Where?"

"I want you to wait in my vehicle before your toes fall off."

"But what are you going to do?"

"Call the local cops and check your house."

She looked back to her home and saw a figure standing on her porch, watching her. "There," she pointed with a gasp. "Look!"

He spun, his hand going to his weapon. "Get in the car!" He shoved her toward it. "Angel, come!" He and the dog took off after the person who'd disappeared.

Teeth chattering, skin pebbled with goose bumps, Kate clutched her pup and stumble-walked toward the SUV, desperate to get some feeling back in her feet. November in Bozeman, Montana, was nothing to play with. It was *cold*.

She opened the door to the vehicle and slid inside. The SUV was off, but the interior was definitely warmer than outside. She slapped the locks and tried to see where her rescuer had gone. If she'd had shoes and a coat, she'd have followed him. *Please don't let him get hurt helping me.* She kept her gaze locked on the direction he'd run in.

Seconds later, a knock on the window startled her, and she bit her lip on a scream. The figure standing there, dressed in a red robe and hunting hat, was someone she'd seen earlier when she'd been moving her meager belongings into the rental. He'd been carrying groceries into the little house next door to hers and had offered a short wave before disappearing inside.

She cracked the SUV's window, not willing to open the door to the stranger. A gust of wind set her teeth to chattering again. "Hi."

"Are you all right?" the man asked.

"I think so."

"Who are you and what's going on out here?"

"My name's Kate." She shot another look at her house. The person was gone and so was Lucas. But where? "I'm renting the house next door to you a-and someone broke in and—"

He blinked. "Broke in?"

"Yes. I ran and there was an officer…and… he… I…" She snapped her lips shut knowing she wasn't making any sense.

"Come on, Kate. You can wait inside my house. It's a lot warmer than the car. You can bring the dog, too."

"O-okay. Thank you." Kate followed the man into his kitchen and blessed warmth flowed over her. "I need to call the cops, make sure the officer helping me has backup." Her neighbor's salt-and-pepper hair stood on end, and his glasses sat crooked on his thin nose. "Please, may I use your phone?" she asked.

She snuggled Cocoa closer and tried to control her trembling. She was safe for the moment, but what about the officer? Lucas.

Her neighbor gave a low grunt then walked to the end table next to the sofa and grabbed an old cordless handset. He thrust it at her. "Here."

Kate punched in 911 then walked to the window to peer out. Inky blackness greeted her beyond the well-lit porch. Her adrenaline continued its path through her body while her muscles bunched against the remembered terror.

"911, what's your emergency?"

"Someone broke into my house. There's an officer chasing the intruder and I think he probably needs backup."

"You're out of the house?"

"Yes."

The clicking of a keyboard reached her through the line. "I have units responding to that area," the woman said. "Did the intruder have a weapon?"

"I didn't stick around to find out." She paused. "But he might be bleeding. He was smothering me, and I grabbed a letter opener and stabbed him with it." The memory sent a fresh wave of horror through her, and a tear dripped off her chin. She swiped it away in an impatient gesture. Would she never be free of this living nightmare? It had been months since her accident, the coma, the therapy—and now this.

"Good job. Stay with me until someone gets there."

Kate looked back at her Good Samaritan neighbor. He'd straightened his glasses and smoothed down the puff of graying hair, but his eyes were wide behind the lenses. "You stabbed him?"

"With a letter opener. He was suffocating me."

The old man's face paled, and he walked to the counter, muttering about people these days and wondering what the world was coming to.

Kate wiped the tears from her cheeks and let out a low breath of relief when the faint sound of the sirens reached her. But what about Lucas Hudson? Was he all right?

She pulled the curtain aside once more and caught sight of flashing blue lights. "They're almost here," she said into the phone.

"Don't hang up yet. Wait until they pull in."

She did so. Less than sixty seconds later,

she hung up and turned to the neighbor. "Thank you. The officers are here."

He handed her a cup of coffee. "I think you might need this. It's that fast stuff from the newfangled machine my daughter got me, but it's pretty good." He shot her a half smile. "Just don't tell her I said so if you ever meet her."

Kate wrapped her hands around the warm mug. Tears clogged her throat at his kindness, and she swallowed hard. "That's very thoughtful. Thank you."

"Welcome. Be careful. It's steaming hot."

Kate took a tiny sip and closed her eyes. Yes, that helped. After another swig that burned all the way down, she opened the door to greet the officers walking toward her. Lucas and Angel appeared as well. But no intruder in sight.

Lucas stepped up beside her as the officers introduced themselves as Brown and Weston.

"Come back inside and shut the door," the neighbor said. "I'll just make myself scarce while you guys take care of business." He got them settled in his den, which smelled like mint and moth balls, then did as he had said he would and vanished into the kitchen. Over the next several minutes, Kate told the officers and Lucas exactly what happened. It didn't take long. "The whole thing probably lasted two or three minutes." But it had seemed like a lifetime.

"Angel and I went after them," Lucas said, "but he disappeared somewhere in the neighborhood. I couldn't send Angel after him because she didn't have any scent article to go by."

"Okay," Officer Weston said. "We'll check the house and be right back."

They left and Kate pressed a hand to her pounding head then looked up to meet Lucas' gaze. "I don't understand."

"What?"

"How he found me."

"I don't know, either," Lucas said, "but looks like we need to find you another place to hide."

Lucas looked at this woman who'd been through so much in the past seven months. He'd been surprised when Detective Skylar Morgan had called him and asked him to check in on Kate Montgomery. He'd been in the area running a specialized training program with his Search and Rescue K-9, Angel, so it hadn't taken him any time to zip over to Kate's location.

"Kate?" he'd asked Skylar. "The Kate from the car accident who was in a coma and woke up without her memory? That Kate?"

"That's the one."

"Yeah, sure, I can do that." He'd had a soft spot for the woman ever since he'd been assigned to find the baby who'd gone missing while in her care. With her remembering more and more of what happened the night someone had run her off the road and left her for dead after setting fire to her car in order to kidnap three-month-old Chloe Baker, Kate might be open to talking to him about the case.

"Thanks."

So, he'd hung up and rushed over only to come upon her running barefoot from the house, terrified out of her mind.

He had recognized her from her pictures and his occasional visit to her bedside when she was still unconscious. He'd noted she was too thin but definitely as pretty as he remembered her with her curly brown hair framing her face and chin.

She bit her lip. "Another place to hide? Really?"

"I don't see that you have any other choice."

She sighed. "Sure, okay. Why not?"

Her weariness touched him, and his heart

went out to her. She looked so alone and scared. And he wanted to help her, which sent a pang of worry colliding with his protective instincts. He put the brakes on any emotional tug he might feel toward her. Hadn't he learned the hard way that doing anything more than his job was an invitation for trouble? Kate was an assignment, nothing more. He'd keep her safe, get her back to her life and move on with his. Period.

He scratched Angel's ears, and she turned her head to swipe his hand with her tongue. He smiled, his love for the animal strong. She was more than a good dog. She was his friend, his partner—and she loved him unconditionally. At least he never had to worry about her leaving him for...

He cleared his throat, realizing Kate was staring at him, waiting on him to tell her his plan. Unfortunately, he didn't have one. His phone buzzed, and he snagged it from the clip on his belt, grateful for the timely interruption. "Hello?"

"It's Skylar. You hadn't checked in about Kate so thought I'd call."

Lucas flicked a glance at Kate who watched him with a frown.

"Yeah," he said, "we've been a little busy."

"Meaning?"

"Meaning it's a good thing you asked me to check in on her."

"Details please?" Tension made her words sharp.

"Angel and I were leading a training session that turned into the real thing. We found some teens that had gone missing, and I was just getting ready to head back to the hotel when you called. I was only about twenty minutes away from Kate's rental and headed over."

"And?"

"She was in trouble." He explained the situation and saw a shudder ripple through Kate as she listened to his side of the conversation. "Thankfully," he said, "she managed to escape about the time I drove up, so she's safe at the moment. The officers are checking things out, but we've got to get her out of there, and she's going to need someone to help her do that."

"And that someone is you." She knew it as well as he did, so her words weren't a question.

"Looks like it. I'll have to swing by the hotel and grab some things and arrange a place for her to stay."

"Where?"

"Not a hundred percent yet, but I'll figure something out."

Skylar sighed. "She said she needed to get away and was drawn to that area. I made it happen for her, but now you're telling me she's been found and attacked."

"In a nutshell—yes."

"Well, that's just great." She paused. "Wait a minute. I might have an idea about where she could go, but you'd have to get her there."

"I can do that."

"I have friends who are converting their cabin into a duplex rental. It's what I originally had in mind for Kate, but it wasn't ready when she wanted to move out to Montana. Now it is and she was supposed to head up there tomorrow. It's about an hour away from where you are now. Just follow the interstate until you come to the small town of Sercy. You'll know it when you see it. It looks like an Old West town. The sheriff there is good friends with the people who own the cabin. He's a good man. Check in with him and let him know what's going on. Anyway, drive through town and go up the mountain. It's pretty remote, but where the cabin is situated—in a large open piece of land—you'd definitely be able to see someone coming. You have your satellite phone?"

"Of course."

"Good. I don't think there's much of a cell signal up there, but if you have the sat phone, you should be fine. I'll make the arrangements and get back to you." She gave him the address and he mapped it on his phone with an app.

"Okay, that looks like it would work," he said. "I still have some training to finish up with another group, but that's at the Sercy High School football field, only about a thirty-minute drive from the cabin, so I know exactly where you're talking about. The only problem is I'll have to leave Kate alone while I do the training, but if no one knows where she is for sure this time, it won't be a problem. Or..." He chewed on his bottom lip while he thought.

"Or?"

"Or she could come with me," he said. Kate's eyes widened slightly, but she looked curious. "Might be boring for her, but she'd be safe surrounded by law enforcement."

At the word *safe*, she relaxed a fraction.

Skylar was quiet, and Lucas figured she was mulling over his words. "I like that," she finally said.

"What? Her going with me?"

"Yeah. See what she thinks about that."

"She's listening—and now nodding. So, I think that's the plan. And after the training is finished, keeping her safe would require me hanging out here in Montana a bit longer."

"I can run it by Tyson and see what he says, but I don't think he'll have a problem with it—especially if it helps us find that missing baby. Chloe Baker is still out there somewhere. I feel sure of it."

"I think this is going to take us one step closer to doing that." Lucas had been a part of the Rocky Mountain K-9 Unit—a unique mobile unit under contract with the FBI—for a year. For the past eight months, he and the others in the unit had been working nonstop to find the missing Chloe Baker, who'd disappeared the night of the car accident that left Kate with amnesia. Chloe had been three months old at the time she'd disappeared. All clues had been pursued and led to multiple dead ends. Their only hope for locating the baby had dwindled to Kate remembering that night.

They'd also been actively searching for the serial killer who they'd finally managed to capture last month. When Lucas had been asked to lead a training mission in Montana this week, Tyson Wilkes, his boss, had told him to go.

"Did you send Kate here knowing I'd be close by?" he asked Skylar.

"Um…no. I mean, not really. When she thought going out to Sercy would be beneficial to regaining her memory, I'll admit to thinking the fact that you were close by only be considered a bonus. Looks like I was right."

"You were."

"All right," she said, "give me ten to twenty minutes to check with my friend and clear everything with Tyson, and I'll get back to you."

"Of course. We'll start heading in that direction. We won't get too far that we won't be able to turn around and find a hotel for the night should we need to."

"Perfect."

"Talk to you soon." He hung up and looked at Kate who held her little dog snuggled up against her. Her fingers stroked the fur in a steady rhythm that seemed to offer her comfort as the lines on her face had faded a fraction. "You two ready to go?" She gave a hesitant nod. "How fast can you be ready to leave?"

"I just need to get my things from the rental," she said. "I could use some help getting my art supplies into the car."

"Of course." He remembered Skylar mentioning Kate was a gifted, well-known, wildlife artist.

"I'll also need to change clothes. Shoes would probably be a good idea, and..." She shrugged. "That's it. So, maybe fifteen minutes?"

"I'll go with you and wait on Skylar to get back to me while you pack."

"What about my car? I'll have to drive it."

"I'd rather you ride with me," he said. "I'll get a couple of the deputies to follow us out to the county line of Sercy and see if the sheriff will meet up with us and trade off. Once they switch drivers, they can ride back together."

"You know the sheriff?"

"No, but I know how to introduce myself."

He shot her a tight smile and she sighed. "That seems like a lot of trouble. I can drive my car."

"If you're driving alone and the person is watching, then he may feel brave enough to initiate another attack. However, if you're with me in a clearly marked law enforcement vehicle, I think it would be more of a deterrent to anyone who might be inclined to follow."

She looked like she might like to offer a rebuttal to that, and Lucas readily admitted it sounded weak on his part. Not that everything he said wasn't true, but more than that, he wanted to talk to Kate. The time in the car together would allow him to pump her for more information about the attack tonight and the night she was almost killed.

The night baby Chloe disappeared while in her care.

"All right," she finally said. "Thank you." She walked over to the older gentleman leaning against the stove and hugged him. "And thank you for your help."

The man blinked rapidly then gave Kate an awkward pat on her back. "You just be careful and stay safe."

"That's the plan."

Then she was exiting through the door with Lucas right behind her. He could only pray his idea was a good one and he could keep her safe from the people who wanted her dead.

TWO

In the SUV, with her minuscule amount of belongings in the back, Kate absently stroked Cocoa's soft fur—a habit she'd quickly developed after Cocoa was placed in her care. For some reason, running her fingers through the silky softness eased the panic that often hovered over her.

Lucas talked on the phone with Skylar and it sounded like everything was arranged for them to stay at the place Skylar knew about. Then he moved on to a call with the sheriff of Sercy, who agreed to help transport her car and finish the escort to the cabin.

When he hung up, the dog in the back stuck her head over the back seat and nudged Kate. Kate let out a low breath she hadn't realized she'd been holding then reached up to scratch the animal's ears. "She's beautiful."

"Thanks. Her name's Angel."

"Hi, Angel. This is Cocoa." She lifted the little dog to face Angel, and Angel studied the mutt for a moment before leaning in for a sniff. Cocoa barked and her tail wagged furiously. Angel flinched back then came back for another smell before she swiped Cocoa's face with her long tongue. Cocoa barked again and Kate laughed. "She loves other dogs."

"Angel's a little more reserved, but, as you can see, it doesn't take her long to warm up. She'll get along fine with Cocoa."

Kate set Cocoa back in her lap. "Skylar convinced me I needed her as an emotional support animal after everything that happened."

"Skylar's a good person to listen to. You've really been through it. First the car wreck and then the coma, then waking up with a foggy memory. Months of therapy... It's no wonder you needed some companionship." He paused. "Has it helped having her?"

"Immensely." She didn't know how she would have functioned without the dog.

He nodded to the GPS on the dash. "Skylar told me a little more about her friend's home. I think you'll like it."

"I'll like any place where I feel safe," she said. "Ever since that night, I feel like I can't get a full breath or do anything without watching over my shoulder. And now with the attack at the rental..." She shook her head.

He glanced at her. "Have you remembered anything else about the wreck?"

"Some. More now than when I first woke up from the coma."

"That's progress."

Not as much as she would have liked.

"Can you tell me what you remember? I've read the report, of course, but I'd rather hear it firsthand from you, see if you can fill in any blank spots."

"Unfortunately, there are a lot of blank spots in my head. For a long time after I woke up, I couldn't remember much of anything. But it's slowly coming back to me. Now I can remember everything about my life right up until the accident. And there are some flashes that I get sometimes from the actual night of the wreck. I also remember pink. Like a sea of pink."

"A sea of pink? What was that?"

"I'm guessing it has something to do with Chloe because her mother, Nikki, always dressed her in pink. I also think I remember the car burning, the smell of smoke and... something else. I don't know what the smell was—something chemical maybe? But the feel of intense heat is very vivid. Almost overwhelming. I feel like I'm suffocating when I dream about it." Try as she might, Kate couldn't remember why she'd been taking care of the woman's baby. Nikki had been found dead in her own car not far from the scene of Kate's accident. The RMKU was investigating but there were few answers.

Lucas reached over and covered her hand with his. "I'm sorry," he said. "That's awful."

"Yeah," she whispered, "it is." But his touch ignited something deep within her. A feeling she couldn't remember having in a very long time.

Safety. Security. Comfort.

Until she remembered that he was just taking her to a safe place then leaving. She pulled her hand from his to rake her hair back into a ponytail that she secured with the band from around her wrist. "I know your team has been searching for Chloe and whoever took her, but I also feel like if I could just access the memories I know are in my head, I could help the process along."

"I'm still not real clear on what you remember and don't remember."

"I'm not exactly clear on it myself. Like I said, I remember lots of pink. And I know that Chloe was with me in the car. I just don't know how she got there. It's weird," she said, pressing a hand to her forehead. "I don't know why I remember some things and not others. If I could just bring those few days leading up to the wreck to the surface, then I think I could answer a lot of questions."

"It's the severe concussion. The more you heal, the more you'll remember."

"That's what they tell me," she murmured.

"So, why are you here in Montana?" he asked. "Why leave all that's comfortable and familiar in Denver?"

She shook her head. "Well, familiar is accurate. Comfortable is stretching it." He nodded and she sighed. "I honestly don't know, but I keep having the feeling that there's something here in Montana. Something I'm supposed to know but can't bring out of my damaged brain. Something Nikki told me or…something. I just can't quite grasp the memory no matter how hard I try." She drew in a ragged breath. "But I'm here now, thanks to Skylar's help, so maybe…with time…it'll come to me."

"It probably will. Don't force it."

"You sound like my therapist. But I'm not pushing. Not too hard, anyway. It's impossible not to keep trying." She paused. "You were going to tell me about this place you're taking me."

"Skylar said it's the place she originally had in mind for you, but it wasn't ready until now."

"Yes, I was just spending the one night in the rental then was to head up the mountain in the morning."

"Well, you'll be a little early, but that's okay. It's about an hour's drive from Billings and the land is just a little over twenty-one acres. It cozies up to acreage that extends all the way to Yellowstone National Park. Granted, the park is about an hour from the cabin, but I'm just giving you the description so you can kind of picture the wide-open spaces."

"Sounds amazing."

He raised a brow at her. "The thought of being so far away in a remote area doesn't bother you?"

"Well, the purpose in being remote is to be able to see who's coming from all sides, right? So no one can sneak up on me, right? I like that idea. Tell me more."

He shrugged. "You've got the views of the Beartooth Mountains to your west, and there's the Clarks Fork of the Yellowstone River Valley to your east. There's also views of the Pryor Mountains. Gotta be careful, though. The wildlife is just that. Wild. You know how to use a rifle?"

"I do. My father used to take me skeet shooting when I was a teenager."

"How's your aim?"

"I won a few competitions."

"You competed?"

"I did." She didn't elaborate and was thankful that he didn't ask. Not that she had anything to hide—she just didn't like thinking about the way she grew up. Everything her parents had lavished her with had been connected to strings. Strings they'd wanted to manipulate to make her dance like their puppet. She gave a soft sigh. That was probably a bit harsh, but nevertheless, it was her perception. They still didn't know about her current situation. The fact they hadn't tried to get in touch with her in seven months showed just how seriously their relationship had degraded.

"Well…good," he said. "Then keep it with you if you go exploring."

What? Oh, the rifle. "Of course, but I doubt I'll do much exploring." Which bothered her. She'd never been one to shy away from hiking and being out in nature discovering new areas to watch the wildlife. She used to spend hours outside sketching and painting any creature who crossed her path.

And now, with someone out to kill her for whatever reason, the thought of going off on her own scared her. And that infuriated her. She wasn't going to let this person win. Fighting back and finding Chloe were her goals right now. Those, and staying alive, of course. "What about you?" she asked. "Where are you staying?"

His gaze locked with hers. "Right now, I'll be staying with you."

She blinked. "Sorry?"

"Well, close by anyway. The cabin is a duplex. You'll be on one side. I'll be on the other. But there's a connecting door, so if you run into trouble, I'll be right there."

"You're not leaving?"

"Like I told Skylar, I've got another two days of training to finish up. So, I'll be around for at least that long. I have a feeling my sergeant, Tyson Wilkes, will be open to me staying longer."

And just like that, she could breathe again. For the next two days at least, she wouldn't be alone and afraid, anxiety eating at her before she reminded herself to pray, and even then, feeling like her prayers were bouncing off the ceiling. But maybe God had heard her and sent Lucas to be her help. "That's…really amazing," she said around a tight throat. "I don't know what to say other than thank you." She frowned. "So, when you finish the training, if you're not approved to stay longer, you'll have to go back to Denver?"

He slid her a smile before he looked back at the road. "Yes, but you're a part of the case that I'm working on, Kate. I think, after tonight, I can't see how anyone can think it would be a good idea for you to be out here alone."

Kate didn't want to start blubbering her relief, but she was right on the edge. "Thank you," she whispered. "I keep saying that, I know, but I mean it."

"I know you do, but you don't have to keep saying it."

"Thank—" She laughed. "I can't help it."

He smiled and, for the first time in a long time, she allowed herself to hope. Maybe, with him beside her and Cocoa in her lap, she could sleep without having a nightmare.

Maybe.

When they reached Sercy, they pulled into the edge of town where the deputies traded off and then they were back on the highway.

"One other thing," he said.

"Yes?"

"The training I'm doing? I think you should go with me."

She blinked at him. "I heard you mention that idea on the phone with Skylar. What would I do?"

"Well, that's the thing. The training day is about six hours with breaks for the dogs and handlers scattered throughout. You could watch, or you could bring your art supplies and paint or draw."

She chewed on her bottom lip. "Well, I don't mind going to the training, but if I'd be a distraction or something, then I'd just prefer to stay wherever we're going."

He shot her a smile, and she gulped. She had no idea why she was noticing it, but she *really* liked his smile—and having it aimed in her direction. And she *really* didn't need to notice that. She had no room for attraction in her life. For a variety of reasons. Not the least of which was the fact that someone had just tried to kill her.

"You wouldn't be a distraction at all," he said. "We need a lot of room when we train, so we use the Sercy High School football field. With all of the law enforcement officers around, I'd think you'd be very safe."

She couldn't deny she liked the sound of that. "Okay, sure. They won't say anything to anyone about me being there, right?"

"Not a word. I'll make sure of it."

"Then that's what we'll do."

"Good. Now, take a deep breath and relax. We're on the flat road for another couple of miles then it's going to get more winding as we climb."

"That's fine. It won't bother me."

"Then maybe you should try to sleep. We'll be there in about forty minutes."

With the plans made, Kate closed her eyes and sent up prayers of gratitude to the Lord for bringing Lucas along at just the right time. *And please, God, watch over Chloe. Keep her safe and help us find her. Soon. Thank you for keeping me alive. I know you have plans for me beyond this, and I really want to fulfill—*

"Kate?"

Her eyes popped open at the sudden tension in his voice. "What is it?"

"Someone's coming up on our tail awful fast and it's not the deputy who was following us in your car. Hold on."

"What do you mean, 'coming up fast'? You mean like to run us off the road?" It was sad her mind immediately went there, but after all that had happened over the last few months, she wasn't going to blame herself for the thought.

"I don't know." But his eyes alternated between the mirrors and the road. He sped up, and Kate clutched the plastic handle attached to the roof above the door. "Actually," he said, "yes, I think so. Hold on." He pressed the gas, and the SUV leaped forward.

Kate kept her gaze centered on the side mirror. "He's getting closer," she whispered. Not that he needed to tell him, but...

"I see him."

The vehicle behind them put on a burst of speed, closed in on the bumper and rammed it. Kate jerked forward against the seatbelt then slammed back against the seat with a gasp while her gaze landed on the animal in their path.

"Lucas! A deer!"

Lucas hit the brake to slow. The deer bounded left, and Lucas whipped the steering wheel to the right. He hit the flat grassy area that ran alongside the highway. They bounced out into the open field and the dogs barked, but he missed the deer. Lucas pressed the brakes once more, and the SUV rolled to a quick stop. He grabbed his weapon. "Stay down and call

911. I have no idea where the other two deputies are. Hopefully, not too far behind."

"What are you doing?" She snagged the
phone and punched in the numbers with shaking fingers. "Can't we just keep going?"

"Blew a tire when I hit the brakes."

Great. *Please, Lord...*

He shoved the door open and took up a position behind it, allowing it to be his cover.
Kate turned to check on the dogs and saw
their harnesses had done the job of keeping
them in the seat. While they'd been startled
by the brief, rough ride, they weren't hurt.

She turned her attention back to Lucas—
and the car that had come to a stop behind
them, headlights aimed in their direction.

Lucas squinted against the bright lights but
kept his weapon aimed at the vehicle. The
truck rolled closer.

"Stop! Stay back!" He honestly didn't know
if the driver could hear him, but the truck
stopped, and he could make out the elbow
propped on the door. "What do you want?"

The engine revved, and Lucas tensed even
more. Would he try to run them down? Crash
the truck into *his* vehicle? Why just sit there
and not say anything?

"My backup is on the way!" His shout echoed in the vast emptiness around them. Two cars shot past them, following the highway, but no one stopped to investigate.

"They're five minutes out," Kate said.

A lot could happen in five minutes.

Kate's car came into sight, and the officer who'd been following them hit his lights.

The truck's engine roared once more and rolled backwards, the wheels screeching when they hit the asphalt. Then it sped away.

Lucas let out a slow breath and holstered his weapon. He glanced at Kate who'd scrunched down in the seat and was holding the phone to her ear. "You okay?" he asked her.

She nodded, her features pale but her jaw set. "You?"

"Yeah."

The officers arrived, and Lucas glared at the one climbing out of Kate's car. "Where were you?"

"Sorry, man. I got cut off about a mile back."

Lucas frowned. "You think they were working together?"

"No, I recognized the driver. It was old man Cagney. He drives slower than my grandma, and I couldn't get around him. When I heard the call come over the radio, I nearly had a heart attack." He tapped the radio on his shoulder. "Sorry about that."

Lucas let it go and gave them a description of the truck as best he could but was disappointed he hadn't gotten the license plate. "Great." He sighed and gestured to the tire. "Help me out?"

"Sure thing." They got the tire changed in record time and soon Lucas found himself back in the driver's seat, heading down the road, the officers close on his tail at this point.

"You told them what was going on?" she asked.

"Enough for them to be more alert and make sure we don't have anyone following for real this time."

She yawned and nodded. "I'm sorry for all the trouble tonight."

He reached over and gave her hand a slight squeeze. "None of this is your fault, so please don't feel like you need to apologize. We have about another twenty minutes to go. I don't expect any more trouble, so close your eyes and try to rest."

"Rest? Not likely."

"Try?"

She sighed. "Sure." She shut her eyes, and they popped back open. "You think he would have done something more if the police hadn't been so close?"

"I don't know." He didn't, but probably. The guy had timed his attack just right, and if the other officers hadn't been behind them, things wouldn't have ended well. At all.

"I'm glad you keep a satellite phone in your car." She sounded sleepy, and Lucas decided to just keep talking to her if that would help her wind down.

"Oh yeah. It's a necessity in this part of the country."

She didn't respond, and he looked over to see her eyes shut, facial features finally relaxed except for the dip between her brows.

"Kate?" He kept his voice low, soft.

She didn't stir and he smiled. Then frowned. Why was he so attracted to the woman? Had he not learned his lesson the hard way? He had a fast and strict rule: do not get emotionally involved with anyone he had rescued. And while Kate wasn't his typical rescue with Angel, she still fit in that category. *Forget it and focus. Keep her safe and move on.*

He pressed the gas and mentally reviewed what he needed to do the next day.

A little less than twenty minutes later, Lucas pulled to a stop at the duplex cabin and cut the engine. The officers rolled up behind him, and he motioned for the one with Kate's car to pull under the lean-to next to the woodshed. He touched Kate's hand and her eyes popped open, a little frantic at first but calmed when she saw him. He had no explanation for the feeling that swept through him at the sight of that. Feelings of a protector, the desire to see her whole and happy and carefree, with the lines of tension around her eyes and mouth gone for good.

He shoved aside the unwelcome thoughts. "Hey."

"I fell asleep?"

"Yeah."

"I have no idea how."

He smiled. "Adrenaline crashes can do that to you."

"I guess."

He let Angel out of the back. She darted off to sniff the surroundings. Her movement triggered outdoor lights, and the place lit up like a Christmas tree.

"Wow."

"Another good safety feature," he said.

"I'm all for safety at the moment." She nodded to Angel. "You don't worry she'll disappear?"

"No way. As soon as I call her, she'll come running."

She smiled. "Cocoa's that way, too. Most of the time. She's still learning, and sometimes it takes me a few calls to get her to come. I can always say the word *t-r-e-a-t*, and she'll head my way." He laughed, and she released the animal from the safety harness and set her on the ground. The little dog shook herself then darted after Angel. "At least they like each other."

"Yeah."

Kate looked at the cabin. "Skylar has very nice friends."

"She does. And she counts you among that special lot." Skylar had acted as a liaison on Kate's case between the Denver PD and the RMKU, but he knew the two women had developed a special bond.

"I know. We've gotten close over the past couple of months. I'm grateful to her."

He shot her a smile and grabbed the bags from the car. "Let's get you settled. You have to be exhausted."

"A bit."

"Hm. More than a bit is my guess."

"You're a good guesser."

Once they said goodbye to the officers,

Lucas led the way to the door, where he punched in the code on the keypad then pushed his way inside. The dogs bounded ahead of them, tongues wagging, sides heaving. "Looks like they had a good run," Kate said. Cocoa flopped on the floor next to the fireplace, and Angel joined her.

"This is your side," he said, setting her bags on the floor. "Skylar sent me the layout and it's simple enough." He pointed to the right. "Down that hallway, there are two bedrooms with a bath in between, and then the rest is what you see. The kitchen has a gas stove, and this den area has the fireplace. No gas there, I'm afraid. I think they plan to convert it, but for now, you need to chop wood for it."

"I prefer to press a button for the flames rather than having to go out in the freezing cold to gather wood, but I'll manage."

"I have no doubt. And I'm here to help. My side is a mirror image. According to Skylar, there are some water bottles in the pantry along with some nonperishables. Staples are in the fridge. That should tide you over until we can do some grocery shopping tomorrow at some point."

"It'll be fine, thanks." She nodded to the animals. "Look at that." Angel had her snout between her paws, and Cocoa was curled up next to her. "I have a feeling the dogs are going to be hanging out together when they're not working."

Lucas smiled. The peaceful scene was… cozy. *Too* cozy. It made him long for things better left "unlonged" for. He cleared his throat. "I'll be next door if you need anything. Just holler. You can lock the connecting door if it will make you feel better, but I promise not to enter unless I have your permission."

Her eyes softened as she looked at him. "If Skylar says I can trust you, then I can trust you. I'm fine with leaving the door unlocked."

Her simple faith in him did more for his heart than he wanted to admit. "Thanks."

Curiosity flickered. "What about you? This is a last-minute change of plans for you. I'm sorry I've disrupted your life. Are you sure this is okay?" The concern behind her question touched him, and it took effort to pull his thoughts together. What was wrong with him? He'd spent a few hours in her company and was being sucked in by her innocence and vulnerability.

Yeah, he'd fallen for that once. Never again. Not that he thought she was faking it. No, even to his jaded outlook, Kate was the real deal. He just wasn't willing to risk his heart ever again. On anyone.

"No," he said, aware the silence had lengthened to an awkward point. "I was…ah…married a couple of years ago, but she decided to move on to greener pastures." And now he wanted the floor to open up and swallow him whole. Why had he just blurted that out? He didn't talk about Shana or his brief marriage. Ever.

Her eyes widened. "Oh, I'm sorry. How awful."

He waved a hand. "It's okay. I guess I was just making the point that you don't need to worry about my personal life. I don't have anywhere to be other than here. My life is my job now and I like it that way." Protest too much? Lucas ignored the taunting inner voice. "All that to say, I'll be next door if you need anything."

Kate offered him a tremulous smile. "Thank you. I appreciate it." She sighed and looked around. "It doesn't look like I have much moving in to do, so I guess I'll let you get back to whatever you were doing before you had to ride to the rescue."

And that was his cue to exit.

So, why did he find himself hesitating? "You sure you're going to be all right?"

"I'll be fine. Knowing you're next door will allow me to really relax and get some much-needed rest."

He could take a hint. He made sure her front door was locked then walked through the connecting door to his side. When he turned to close it, he caught her eyes. "Sleep well, Kate. I promise no one's getting to you as long as I'm here."

She swallowed and nodded. "Thank you," she whispered. "Again." She gave a small laugh. "I'm sorry. I have to say it."

"I know. Good night." He pulled the door shut and pulled in a deep breath. Then realized he'd left Angel on her side of the duplex. With a silent groan, he knocked, and she opened the door with a smile. "Need your dog?" she asked.

"Please."

Once Angel was back with him and he'd shut the door once more, he shook his head. He was going to have to stay focused on the case and keep Kate at arm's length or he was going to be in trouble. Like he'd told her, his job was his life, which meant he had no room for distractions. Especially, not a pretty woman with a faulty memory and someone out to silence her forever.

THREE

Near the end of the second day of training, Kate had to admit she'd enjoyed watching the process more than she thought she would. The Sercy High School football field, about thirty minutes from the cabin, was the perfect place for the exercise, and the past two days had been nothing short of fascinating.

She'd had to leave Cocoa in the temperature-controlled vehicle some of the time, but other times Lucas had used the little dog as a distraction in order to train the other dogs to stay focused. Thankfully, it appeared Lucas had been right, and trouble had left her alone. While she was thankful for that, she knew it meant he'd most likely be returning to Denver first thing tomorrow.

Since it looked like they were wrapping things up, Kate decided she'd visit the restroom, take Cocoa for one last walk and be ready when Lucas was. Kate noticed the closer they got to leaving, the more her nerves stretched. She didn't relish being alone, hiding out, trying to stay safe while Lucas and his team tried to figure out who was after her and why, but she'd manage. She had this long, right?

She motioned to Lucas, who was talking to one of the trainees, that she was heading to the little building with the restrooms and he nodded. Most of those involved with the training had already packed up and left. School would be letting out soon, and the football team would need the field.

At the restroom, she slipped inside. She headed for the nearest stall when something jammed into the side of her back, and she froze. "I've been waiting all day for you to come in alone."

Terror blindsided her. "What do you want?"

"You. Let's go."

"Wh—why?"

A knock on the door made them both jerk, and she sucked in a ragged breath.

"Kate?" Lucas's voice sounded from the other side. "I'm going to let Cocoa out. You okay?"

She stayed silent.

The gun jabbed once more. "Answer him."

"Kate?"

"Um, yes. I'll be, um, just a minute."

"Okay—"

"Help!" She spun, praying he wouldn't pull the trigger. Her left forearm connected with his, and he gave a grunt of pain. The gun clattered to the floor.

Kate dove for it, reacting out of instinct more than skill.

The man behind her cursed and shoved her hard. She slammed into the side of the stall, and a cry slipped from her.

The door burst open, and Lucas filled the doorway. "Kate!"

She rolled in time to see her attacker barrel into Lucas and send him to the floor. Then he was gone, and Lucas was scrambling to his feet. He looked over his shoulder then back at her. "Are you okay?"

"Yes." In shock, but okay.

"I'm going after him. You stay put. Stay here and lock the door behind me."

She sucked in a breath and nodded while Lucas called it in and took off out the door. She locked it then turned and leaned against it. Her shoulder hurt where she'd rammed it against the stall, but other than that, she was unhurt.

But Lucas…

Time passed while she tried to figure out what to do. Go after Lucas or stay put like he told her to?

Someone rapped on the door, and she gasped. "Who is it?"

"It's me, Kate," Lucas said. "You can open the door."

She flipped the lock and pulled it open. He stood there, windblown and frowning, but at least he was in one piece. "He got away. I couldn't send one of the dogs after him because I didn't have any kind of scent article. What happened?"

"He said he was waiting on me. That he'd been waiting to get me alone." She hated the tremble in her voice and cleared her throat. "He had a gun and when you knocked on the door, I just reacted. I couldn't let him send you away, but I was afraid if you came in, he might shoot you." She ran a shaky hand over her hair. "He dropped the gun and it slid under the stall."

"Seriously?" He shot her a tight smile. "Good. I'll get an evidence bag, and we'll see if the lab can pull any prints."

"He had on gloves."

"I know, but we'll hope for the best." He reached for her hand. "Come on. We need to get back to the cabin where it's safe."

"How do you think he found this place? How did he know I'd be here?"

"I don't know. When we catch him, I'll ask him. But I know one thing. This just goes to prove someone is going to a lot of trouble to get to you."

"I wish I knew who."

"So do I." He paused. "What if it's someone who's afraid you can identify them?"

"Identify them from what?"

"The night of the accident? When Chloe disappeared?"

She frowned. "It's possible, I suppose." She clenched her fists. "In that case, I need to remember faster than ever."

"Let's get back to the cabin. I'll have one of the sheriff's deputies follow us like before and make sure we're not being tailed."

She nodded and slipped out the door just behind Lucas. It didn't take him long to grab an evidence bag and slip the weapon inside it. He labeled it and asked the nearest deputy to be sure it was delivered into the right hands.

The woman promised to do so.

Once Kate was buckled in the passenger seat, she leaned her head back against the headrest and closed her eyes. And a memory surfaced. Just out of nowhere, it played like a movie in her head, and she gasped.

"Kate?"

"I remembered something." Goosebumps pebbled her arms.

"What?"

"Chloe's mother, Nikki. It's about Nikki and the day of the…incident."

"Tell me."

"I've known Nikki since childhood. She was also my college roommate. She called me. We'd had lunch that day, and I'd kept Chloe for her for a couple of hours so she could go to a doctor's appointment. Everything seemed fine at lunch. Chloe was content and slept through most of it, then she and I took a walk and did some window-shopping before Nikki came to get her. But just a few hours later, Nikki called. She was desperate. Frantic. She told me she needed me, and I immediately agreed to help her. She wouldn't go into details on the phone but gave me directions to meet her."

"Directions to where?"

"A very isolated place in the middle of a

national park. She said she wanted some-where out in the open so she could tell if any-one was following her. She let me know she'd be in disguise and wearing a blond wig. Of course, this raised all kinds of alarms for me, but I went because she was my friend, and she was in trouble."

"Nikki was found wearing the wig," he said. "And some hairs from it had been on the infant car seat and baby blanket near your car." He nodded. "Then what happened?"

"I got there, but it was dark and creepy, and I really wanted to just leave. But I didn't. I couldn't. Nikki had been the closest thing to a sister that I had as a child, my best friend and college roommate, and she'd reached out to me for help. I wasn't going to say no, so I waited for her. I thought I heard her car com-ing down the road. I think I remember head-lights." She stopped, her eyes widening. "I just remembered something else! Nikki *was* there, and she had Chloe with her. Obviously. And Nikki was scared. I remember that."

"Scared of what? Who?"

She closed her eyes, trying to remember. But there was nothing. "No idea." She huffed. "That's one of the gaps in my memory. I don't know what happened between seeing Nikki in her car with the baby to the point where I had Chloe in my car. I mean, obviously, she'd asked me to take the baby, and I'd agreed, but no matter how hard I think or push, I can't figure out who she was so scared of. Truly, I think if we knew that, we'd know who has Chloe."

"We'll keep working on it," he said. "For now, just lean back and catch your breath."

Kate did as he suggested but sent a prayer toward the Heavens. *Lord, please, please help me remember the rest.*

For the next two days, Kate kept a careful watch out the window, but she was starting to think no one knew where she was and that she really *could* let the constant tension in her shoulders release. Not a lot, but maybe a fraction.

After the attack at the football field, Lucas had received permission to stay with her at the cabin for an unspecified period of time. That news went a long way toward improving her mental state.

So much so that, over the past two days, she'd been venturing outside more, exploring the area with the rifle and Cocoa at her side and Lucas not too far in the distance.

A knock on the connecting door pulled her from her thoughts. "Come on in."

Lucas pushed the door open. He was freshly shaven, his hair still damp. He looked decidedly handsome, and once again, she had to remind herself she had no business noticing that. He was her protector, nothing more. The fact that her heart wanted to protest was unsettling.

He held a steaming mug in his right hand and a frown on his face. "Morning," he said.

"Good morning. You look tense. What is it?"

"I got a call from the sheriff."

The hairs on her neck stood up. "About?"

Angel darted around Lucas's legs and made her way to Cocoa's side in front of the fire, where she gnawed a chew toy. The little dog seemed happy to see her new friend and dropped the toy in front of Angel, who gave it a sniff and dismissed it.

"Someone in a house along the route we took the other night said they had some footage of the guy who ran us off the road," Lucas told her. "You can see the driver but not well enough for any kind of facial recognition software to identify him, but the sheriff wants you to take a look at it."

"Of course. You have it on your phone?"

He rubbed his chin and shook his head. "That's the kicker. We have to go into town to see it. He can't get it to send to my email. He's not sure if the problem's on his end or ours. I checked all the connections and the Wi-Fi seems to be working fine, but it might just not be strong enough. I did ask him to drive it out here, but he has back-to-back meetings today." He hesitated. "I feel like this is time sensitive. The sooner we identify this guy, the better. I told him we'd come in." He paused. "And besides, I need dog food for Angel. She's not going to be happy if I run out."

She nodded. "Okay. When do you want to go?"

"As soon as you're ready."

"Give me a few minutes. It won't take me long."

"You got it." He backed up and shut the door while a new energy hummed through Kate's veins. She was more than ready to break free of the cabin and venture into the small town about thirty minutes south of her current location. She wasn't thrilled about the reason, but even that was okay. It was a step in the right direction. Would she recognize the person in the video?

She made quick work of making herself presentable enough to go into town then put a leash on Cocoa, and they stepped outside to greet the fresh air and chill of the November morning. Lucas had pulled his SUV up to the door, and she handed Cocoa to him then climbed into the passenger seat. Angel greeted the little dog like she hadn't seen her in ages.

Kate chewed her bottom lip while she buckled up then caught him watching her. "What are you thinking?" he asked.

"You know I trust you, but I can't help but feel like I'm taking a risk in leaving a safe place."

He aimed the vehicle down the mountain then shot her a glance. "I think that's a valid concern, but let's think this through. On our way to the cabin, we came through town in the middle of the night, so I feel comfortable saying that no one saw us—except for the person who ran us off the road, and I think he'd been following us for a while, just waiting for his chance to strike. There was quite a bit of traffic on the drive, and he waited until we were on a pretty deserted road."

That was true.

"However," Lucas continued, "thanks to the fact that we had an escort, we *know* no one followed us after the incident on the road. I'm still not sure about how the guy found us at the football field." He tapped the steering wheel. "But he'll have no idea we're coming to town today since it's so last minute, so I don't think it's anything to worry about there."

"Okay." She studied him, her heart full of gratitude for his concern and care—and his efforts to ease her anxiety.

"What we'll do," he said, "is go straight to the sheriff's office and watch the video then straight back to the cabin."

She nodded. "I understand."

When they drove into the edge of town, Christmas lights blinked at her, and Kate drew in a breath of appreciation for the area. "It looks like something on a postcard."

He smiled. "I know. You like the city, don't you?"

"I do. How'd you know?"

"I just kind of thought so. I do, too. For a city boy like me, you would think I'd be itching to get back to all the conveniences available there." He shrugged. "But I also love small towns, and I'm going to miss this one when it's time to move on."

Right. Moving on. She couldn't let herself relax her guard or get comfortable with him.

He was only there to keep her from getting killed and being attracted to him would only bring heartache for her. She forced herself to focus on her surroundings instead of the man next to her, and with each building they passed, she found something new to admire. "They could film an old Western movie here and not have to do anything but get rid of the cars and disguise the streetlights."

He laughed. "I figured you would appreciate seeing this."

"I saw a little bit when we passed through on the way up to the cabin, but this is amazing in the daylight." She drew in a breath and let it out slowly, the simple conversation a relief. Talking about Christmas and lights, postcards and movies seemed almost silly in light of everything she was dealing with, but it felt…good. Necessary for her peace of mind.

"You said, 'when it's time to move on.' I know you're supposed to have done that already. So, what would you be doing if you weren't here?" she asked.

"I'd be back to Denver, working with the team and Angel and rescuing people who need it."

His words just reiterated what she already knew. He was a rescuer. A protector.

Gratitude didn't come close to describing her feelings at the moment. Gratitude was fine, she reminded herself. *Attraction* was not. He no doubt knew who her parents were. Her wealthy and connected parents. And whenever men found out who she was related to, they always looked at her with dollar signs in their eyes. Not that Lucas was like that, but once burned...

"Tell me about your team," she said, not wanting to let her mind go down that train of thought. "My conversations with Skylar have been interesting in learning how the unit came together, but she hasn't given me a lot of details about each member."

"The team is amazing. It's truly a collection of some of the best and most talented officers out there."

"Including you."

He shot her a quick smile. "Including me." His eyes shadowed for a brief moment. "We've all worked hard to get where we are, and we've got stories of how we came to be a part of the team. One day I'll share them with you." He drove down Main Street, slow and patient with the morning traffic and pedestrians crossing from one side to the other.

"I'd love to hear them."

"When we have more time," he said. "We're almost there."

"That works." She pointed. "I love that all the stores already have their Christmas decorations up. They're so pretty."

"Thanksgiving is in two weeks."

"I know. I have a lot to be thankful for."

"Like?"

"Being alive for one."

"I like your attitude."

"It's a daily choice right now," she said. Her wry tone brought a smile to his face, and once again, she had to admit, she liked that.

"What about you?" he asked. "What are your plans once all this is cleared up?"

Assuming it ever will be. "I'll go back to focusing on my art. Before the accident, there was a gallery in New York that was interested in having me do a show there. If they're still interested, I think I'd like to do that and see what could come of it."

He shot her a quick glance. "That's amazing."

"Thank you."

His support touched her more than she wanted to admit. And also sent a shaft of pain slicing through her. Why couldn't her parents see that she had to be who she was created to be? An artist who loved the outdoors. Loved the creatures God had designed. He'd gifted her with a unique talent that enabled her to paint those animals and capture their emotions on canvas in such a way that people were captivated by the pieces, which made for good sales for her. She was very successful in her world, but her parents had never been able to accept that—because it wasn't *their* world. She'd defied their plans for her, and they just didn't know what to do with that—or her.

Lucas slowed for the car in front of him, and she watched him from the corner of her eye. Was he as genuine as he came across? She had no doubt that she could trust him to keep her safe physically, but emotionally was a whole other question. The fact that her mind even went there made her frown.

"We're here," he said before she could self-analyze further. "Let me come around and kind of shield you from view."

"Oh. Okay."

When he was next to the door, she opened it and slid out. "We'll leave the dogs here," he said. "They'll be fine. It's temperature controlled."

"Perfect."

He slipped an arm around her shoulders and tugged her close to his side. Kate's breath caught at how natural the whole thing felt. Discounting the reason for it, of course. But she had to admit she didn't mind being in his arms. And that rattled her almost as much as the fact that she had someone trying to kill her. Like she'd been reminding herself over and over, being attracted to her protector could only lead to problems—and she had enough problems at the moment.

The morning was cold, but it wasn't a deterrent to the people out running their errands. Lucas noted most of them were women and children, and the dogs would attract their attention. The less attention, the better, so the dogs would just stay in the vehicle for now.

He breathed a sigh of relief when he managed to get Kate into the office without anyone stopping them to chat or express the curiosity openly displayed in a few of the glances they'd received.

The inside of the sheriff's office felt like home. He was glad to see the modern interior—a direct contrast to the historical exterior. He shut the door, and the fact that he was trying to find an excuse to keep his arm around Kate sent his brain into a tailspin. He released her and cleared his throat.

The woman behind the desk looked up. "Hello. You must be Lucas and Kate. I'm Tris, short for Beatrice. The sheriff said you'd be stopping by." She rose and motioned for them to follow. "This way."

Seconds later, they stepped into the sheriff's small office. "Take a seat," Tris said. "He'll be with you in just a minute."

They settled into the chairs opposite the large mahogany desk laden with papers, manila folders and two computers.

Kate raised a brow. "Why am I surprised that this office is so…"

"Up-to-date? Modern?" Lucas asked when she faltered. "Current in law enforcement technology and practices?"

"Yes. The complete opposite of what it looks like on the outside."

He smiled. "I know. I'm a little surprised, too, but Skylar filled me in. Her friends who own the cabin we're staying at are buddies with the sheriff and his wife. She let him know what was going on and why we were staying there. Apparently, the sheriff has spent some time in a big city and brought all he learned back to his hometown."

"Good for him."

The door opened, and a large man about Lucas's age stepped inside. Lucas stood and shook his hand. "Sheriff Styles."

"Call me Quinn. Thanks for coming down the mountain. Sorry you had to make the trip. We've got all kinds of technology here, but it can go on the fritz occasionally. This morning is one of those times."

"It's not a problem. If Kate can ID the driver, then it's all worth it. And I really appreciate you arranging the trade off with the deputies. I know you had to roll them out of bed."

"They're good people. All I had to do was ask. I hate that you ran into trouble, though. I'll be honest. That concerns me."

It concerned Lucas, too. "Well, it's been two days since the last incident—which was about thirty minutes from here—so I'm hoping we're in the clear."

The sheriff rubbed his hands together. "All right, then. Let's get to it. I've got about twenty minutes before I have to head into a Zoom meeting—assuming our IT guy has everything up and running by then." He grimaced. "I hate those things. Zoom meetings, not the IT guy."

Lucas laughed. "I know the feeling."

"All right, first things first. The sheriff of Bozeman sent me a report." He scowled. "Via fax, obviously, since our email is being wonky." He pushed the paper toward Lucas. "They ran the DNA found on the letter opener Kate used to stab her attacker. Came back as not in the system."

"Of course it did," Kate said. A sigh slipped from her, but her gaze was steady. "What else?"

"Let's see here." The man turned to the computer on his left, tapped a few keys then swiveled the monitor so it faced Lucas and Kate. "This is the video from the security camera. Thankfully, I was able to download it before all our tech issues started. The house has been there since the beginning of time, but the owners keep everything upgraded. Including their security system. Their daughter is one of my deputies and when she heard what happened, but more specifically, *where* it happened, she went looking for this."

"Nice," Lucas said.

The sheriff tapped another button on the keyboard, and the video played.

Kate leaned forward, hand pressed to her lips. Lucas watched the truck zip past the house. More clicking by the sheriff. "I managed to slow it down, and this is what I've got." He brought up a still picture, and Lucas focused on the face of the individual behind the wheel.

"He's got a ball cap on," Kate said, dismay in her tone. "His face is in the shadows."

"I know, but just look at him," Lucas said. "His hands on the wheel, the way he's sitting in the seat. Is there anything familiar about him at all?"

She fell silent, then said, "Yes, actually. He is a little familiar, but…"

"What?"

She shot him a look full of frustration. "I don't know. He… Yes, he looks familiar, but I can't place him." She frowned. "Or her."

"Her?" Quinn frowned. "You think it could be a woman?"

"It's possible." She fell silent, watching to the end. "Can you play it again?"

"Sure." Quinn started the footage rolling once more, and she took over the track pad to pause it at certain frames.

"What are you looking for, Kate?" Lucas asked her after her fourth pass.

"Just reinforcing some thoughts." She pointed. "I don't do a lot of people portraits, but the shape of the jaw is rather soft, and the hands are small. His—or her—head also doesn't come up against the seat rest very far, which, to me, indicates that the person is rather short. So, it could be a woman or a small-boned man."

Quinn blinked at her, his brows drawn tight over the bridge of his nose. He glanced from Kate to Lucas, his silent questions easily read.

"She's an artist," Lucas said. "She sees things in ways we might not—or don't."

Her gaze locked on his, and her frustration softened for a brief moment. "Thanks," she said, her voice soft.

"What about the person in the bathroom who attacked you?"

"I don't know. I was scared, but the voice was low. A whisper. It could have been either male or female. I can't say for sure. But in the video... I don't know. I think it could be a woman."

"A woman, huh? Well, that's just awesome," Quinn said. "Instead of narrowing down the suspect pool, we just doubled it."

"Sorry," Kate said. She worried her bottom lip and kept her eyes on the screen. "I'm not saying it's definitely a woman. Just that it *could* be. But," she nodded at the computer, "I think he—or she—is wearing glasses."

"What?"

"Look at the little bit of reflection from the streetlight in the window. I know the driver had the hat pulled low and the head is tilted to the left, but just beyond, there seems to be a little bit of an outline of a pair of glasses—and maybe a goatee?"

This time the sheriff's brows rose, and he looked at Lucas. "I think I need to hire her. She'd make a good detective."

Kate flushed. "Like Lucas said, I'm an artist. When I look at a picture such as this, it's all about light and shadows and highlights for me."

"Okay, our person has glasses. Good to know." He turned the screen back to face himself. "If you think of anything else—or who this person reminds you of—get back to me ASAP, okay?"

"Of course. I'll keep thinking." She pursed her lips. "Is there a way to get some screenshots and print them out?"

"I can do that. Go through the footage again, save the screenshots to the desktop and I'll get them printed for you."

She did then stepped back when she was finished.

The sheriff studied her a moment. "I know your name. Kate Montgomery."

Kate stilled and her hands twisted in her lap. "Oh?"

"When Lucas said you were an artist, it kind of clicked. Do you do wildlife portraits by any chance?"

"I do."

He nodded. "Thought so. Saw one of your shows in California a couple of years ago. You do amazing work."

"Thank you so much. I'm honored."

"The world needs more good things like your art, so you just keep doing what you're doing. I'm sure your family is proud of you."

She went white and her smile was definitely forced. Lucas's internal radar beeped. The sheriff had hit a touchy subject for her. "Thank you," was all she said then fell silent. He made a note to ask her about the reaction to the mention of her family.

The sheriff leaned in. "Now, Lucas, I'd like to talk to you about something else, if you don't mind."

"What's that?"

"Training. I talked to the leader of the group you just finished with, and he was very complimentary. I've been pushing to get a

K-9 program here, and I think picking your brain might just be the thing."

"Sure, give me some details about what you're thinking."

Kate rose and walked to the window where she stood to the side, looking out. The frown on her face tugged on Lucas's sympathy, but he forced his attention back to the man in front of him. It was hard to focus on the sheriff's words because keeping Kate safe was all he could seem to think about at the moment.

Because he knew without a doubt whoever was after Kate wasn't going to give up until he'd –or she'd—accomplished what he'd set out to do—and that was to see her dead.

FOUR

I'm sure your family is proud of you.

Not exactly, but she refused to get into it with the sheriff. She wished she could push the words out of her head, but they were there, echoing, taunting, maddening. Her parents *should* be proud of her. She'd worked hard and earned every bit of recognition in her field that she'd received. But if her parents were proud—or thought about her at all— she had no way of knowing since they didn't communicate.

"You have a week to come to your senses, Kate," her mother had stated coldly over the phone when she'd learned Kate, in her sopho- more year of college, had changed her busi- ness major to art. "Our family does business, not art. You really think you can make it on your own?"

"I don't know, Mother, but I want to try."

"Ridiculous. If, after a week, you still intend to pursue this foolishness, you're cut off."

The conversation had gone downhill from there, and Kate had hung up, her heart shattered, though she was not surprised by her mother's pronouncement. But Kate was firm in her decision. She'd gone back to her room and spent the night thinking about what her future would be if she gave in simply for financial reasons. And while it was intimidating—and flat-out terrifying—she'd stuck to her guns, cashed in on a small inheritance from her paternal grandparents and gotten loans to cover the rest of her schooling.

She sighed. Now she didn't have many regrets in life, but the rift between her and her parents was one of the biggest.

Another was that she couldn't fully remember the night baby Chloe Baker had been kidnapped. She'd been entrusted to Kate, but why? For reasons that had gotten Nikki killed and left Kate for dead.

"Oh, Chloe, where are you?" The whisper fell from her lips. The baby needed her to focus her full attention on remembering. Shoving aside her parental problems, Kate glanced at the men behind her still talking and planning then turned back to study the details of the general store across the street. Someone had gone to a lot of trouble to give it the late 1880s feel. And they'd succeeded.

She liked the little town and, while she couldn't explain why, she was still drawn to it—or at least this area. For some reason, she *needed* to be here. But why? It seemed like every time she regained a piece of her memory, it just created more questions that she had no answers to. Which just led to more frustration with herself.

The sheriff's office was located on Main Street surrounded by local shops and businesses. She'd noticed the large grocery store and two fast food chain restaurants as they'd driven down the street. From her vantage point, she spotted a diner next to the general store. The full parking area spoke highly of the food, and her stomach rumbled. When was the last time she'd eaten out without worrying someone would try to kill her?

She wasn't sure. Maybe the day before she'd agreed to meet Nikki?

While the sheriff and Lucas talked, she thought about the doorbell footage of the person who'd run her and Lucas off the road. Why did what little she could see of him or her look familiar? Or did they? Could it be she just wanted to remember so desperately that her mind was playing tricks on her and she'd actually never seen the driver before?

She blew out a sigh and focused on Lucas's SUV. Her angle from the window was such that she could see into the vehicle. Cocoa sat in the back looking out the window while Angel rested her head on the armrest in the middle. Kate let her gaze roam, noting the action on the sidewalk and the snowy, slushy street.

A man bundled in a heavy coat, gloves, scarf and hat peddled a bicycle in the narrow bike lane. A woman with a toddler on her hip walked into the fabric store. Two older men with steaming coffee cups settled themselves on the bench in front of the convenience store. The one on the left set his cup on the wooden boardwalk, pulled on his gloves and tugged his hat over his ears. Three teens huddled around a phone laughing and talking.

It all looked so normal, and Kate found herself longing for what they had. None of them had someone out to kill them, and they were just going about their daily lives. Not that their lives were perfect—because no one's was—but she was envious of the fact that they weren't…like her.

She wanted her life back—and that included all of her memories, good and bad.

The man on the bicycle jerked the handlebars and swerved into the street. Horns honked, and he dodged a car only to head straight for Lucas's SUV. He finally braked to a stop, narrowly missing slamming into the vehicle, but he and the bike fell to the ground dropping out of her sight.

Kate gasped. Angel and Cocoa barked.

"Kate?" Lucas stood and joined her at the window. "What is it?"

"A man on a bicycle nearly wiped out with your SUV." A bystander hurried over, and the rider stood. He shook his head and waved off his would-be helper. "He looks okay, though."

When the onlookers realized the guy was unhurt, they continued on their way. The man on the bike, however, walked around to the side of Lucas's vehicle, glanced around and peered in the window. Then pulled on the handle. Kate gaped then turned to Lucas. "Did you see that? Is he trying to get to the dogs?"

Lucas spun toward the door. "Stay here with the sheriff." Before Kate could respond, Lucas had run from the office. She heard the front door slam and debated whether or not to follow. Then turned back to the window to see Lucas dash down the steps.

The man, who had been peering in the window once again with his hands cupped around his eyes, looked up at Lucas's sudden appearance. Kate lifted the window a fraction in order to hear.

"...help you?" Lucas asked.

"Uh...yeah. Sorry, I heard the dogs barking, and I just wanted to... I thought..."

"You thought what?"

The stranger glanced up, and his eyes met hers. The cold hatred there stole her breath. She knew him. But...she didn't. She needed to see the rest of his face, half-hidden behind the scarf. The hat covered his hair, but, like the shadowy figure in the doorbell footage, something about him was familiar. His eyes. She'd seen those eyes before. She needed to talk to him.

"Lucas! I think I know him. Tell him to stay there. I want to come talk to him."

The man cursed and took off.

"Hey! Stop!"

Kate spun from the window, Lucas's shout echoing in her ears. She darted past the startled sheriff and Tris and out onto the front steps of the building just in time to see Lucas head into an alley, Angel at his side.

The man's quickness had caught Lucas by surprise, and in the few seconds it had taken him to let Angel out of the SUV, the guy was turning the corner of the building and heading into the alley. "Federal agent! Stop!"

Of course, he didn't. He made it into the alley, and Lucas could only hope it was a dead end. The backdoor to one of the stores opened, and a woman stepped out carrying a full trash bag. The fleeing figure shoved her aside, and the woman went down with a scream. The bag rolled in front of Lucas, and he managed to jump it and keep going. "Sorry, ma'am!"

Angel bounded after him, enjoying the chase, but he couldn't let her go after the man alone. She was Search and Rescue, not an apprehension K-9. She wouldn't know what to do once she caught up with the guy. The fleeing figure shot out of the front of the store and fled down the sidewalk, dodging people. Lucas pounded after him then caught sight of him disappearing into another alley. Lucas rounded the corner after him then pulled to a stop. This alley ended with a dumpster backing up to a fence. Just like he'd wanted. "Stop! There's nowhere to go. I just want to talk to you."

After a split-second pause, the man looked back, saw Lucas and Angel closing in and scrambled up on top of a dumpster then over the fence. He dropped to the ground with a hard thud then scampered behind the building. Angel skid to a stop with Lucas right behind her. There was no way Angel could scale the fence, and by the time he managed to get her over, the guy would be gone. And he wasn't about to leave her behind.

It was too late to call for backup. Frustration built. Kate had recognized the man and wanted to talk to him, and Lucas had let him get away. "Come on, Angel. We lost him."

The dog swiped his hand with her tongue, and he scratched her ears. He hoped Kate had stayed put with the sheriff like he'd asked. He hurried back to the station and spotted the bicycle behind his SUV. An idea occurred to him, and he walked Angel over to the bicycle seat. "Get a whiff, Angel. Seek."

Angel nosed near the seat, sniffing, getting the scent. The sheriff came to the door, and Kate stood behind him arms crossed, eyes narrowed. "He got away?" she asked.

"He did, but he left his scent behind. I'm going to see if Angel can pick it up." He looked at the sheriff. "We followed him down the alley behind the Mexican restaurant, but he jumped the fence. Angel and I couldn't follow. Where does that come out?"

"At the back of the beauty salon."

"Easiest way to get there?"

"I'll show you."

"No." Lucas almost shouted the word then cleared his throat. "Sorry, but with someone after Kate, I'd really appreciate it if you would stay here with her while Angel and I do our thing. If we find him, I'll call you."

"Hold on a sec." He hurried to Tris's desk and grabbed a radio from a drawer. "Take this. I'll hear anything you say, and so will all of the other deputies. Channel 9."

"Got it. And can you see if there's any footage of the incident on your cameras?" He pointed to the camera on the corner of the sheriff's office facing the parking lot. Quinn nodded. Lucas clicked to Angel, and they ran back down the steps. "I'll be back! Keep her safe."

Lucas let Angel get one more sniff of the seat then he led her down the sidewalk to the alley behind the salon. "Seek, Angel."

Her nose lifted, and she danced sideways,

sniffing. Then her head lowered, and she walked to the fence, spun and darted to the back of the store. She stopped at the door and pawed it then sat. Which meant she wanted to go in. Lucas tried the knob, and it turned under his touch. "Go," he said. "Angel, seek."

She bolted inside, and Lucas followed after her. Angel cut through the storage room and into the main area where three women worked at their hair stations. One glanced up as Angel entered and gaped. "Who are you? What do you want?"

"Sorry," he said, showing her his badge. "Did a man come this way?"

"Yes." She planted her hands on her hips. "What is going on today? All of a sudden, this the route everyone takes to get to Main Street? Gonna have to lock that backdoor."

"Again, sorry." Angel led him out of the store and back onto the sidewalk. She walked a few more paces before she stopped, her head swiveling, nose quivering. "Come on, girl. Seek." She tried once more then dropped her head. Her signal that she couldn't find the scent. He scratched her head. "It's all right, girl. We tried." He radioed the sheriff and let him know Angel had lost the scent but he needed to speak to a witness.

"Kate's fine, just anxious to see you walk back in the door."

"I'll be there shortly."

Lucas hung up. He and Angel returned to the salon and walked inside. The same woman he'd spoken to earlier stopped her cutting and looked up once more. "You again?"

"I was chasing the guy who ran through here. Is there anything you can tell me about him?"

She blinked and rubbed her head. "Well, it happened fast, but I noticed he was kind of short. I don't have any idea what his face looks like since he was all bundled up against the cold with a hat and scarf and all."

He turned to the others who were watching with wide eyes and listening intently. "Anyone else have anything they can add?"

He got the head shakes he expected. "Okay, thank you for your time. Sorry about the disruption." He and Angel headed out the door. The front door this time.

When he walked into the sheriff's office, Kate's pale, worried face was like a punch to his gut. He felt like he'd failed her by allowing the man to escape. "I'm sorry, Kate."

"It's not your fault. You and Angel tried."

Exactly what he'd said to Angel, but it still

stung that they'd lost him. He looked at the sheriff. "Anything on the security footage?"

"It got the incident, but the guy had on gloves and everything. There's no way to tell what he looks like with him all bundled up in his winter gear, or even get prints off the door handle where he grabbed it. Kate took a peek, too, and agrees." The sheriff rubbed the back of his neck. "Although, with the bike in our possession, it's possible the person touched the handlebars before he put on the gloves. I have a fingerprint kit. I'll see if I can find anything. I'll have to send them off to the state lab for reading, but it's worth a try."

"No," Lucas said. "If you can pull some prints, I'll give you the information where to send them. I have access to a lot of FBI resources, and this something we can get expedited."

The sheriff raised his brows. "Okay, I'll let you know if I find anything."

"That would be great," Lucas said. He looked at Kate. "I didn't see any glasses on him. Did you?"

"No," Kate said. "But while I couldn't tell if he had on glasses, I think it was the same person who attacked me in the little rental house."

Quinn frowned. "What makes you say that?"

"I don't know. Nothing specific. Just a feeling." She paused. "Just from that video, it looked like it could have been. However, seeing the man Lucas just chased, the shape of his upper body is very similar. Thin, smaller boned, his left shoulder hunched slightly... It's the same person who was in the house, I feel sure of it. But the person in the car is a woman."

"So, there are two people after you," the sheriff said.

"They're probably working together." Lucas ran a hand over his chin. "This guy must have been hanging around town thinking we'd come in for supplies if we were staying around here."

"Or waiting to see if he could pick up the trail from here to figure out where we'd gone," Kate muttered.

Lucas nodded. "Whichever it was, he got what he was looking for."

"Us?" she asked.

"And the fact that he knows for sure we're staying in the area now. That was pretty smart on his part. But it means he's been staying around here, too." He raked a hand down his cheek, thinking. Finally, he looked at the sheriff. "I have an idea, but it's going to take some man power and legwork."

Quinn tilted his head. "Tell me."

"How many hotels and motels are in this town?"

"Four."

"Campground? RV sites?"

"Nearby? Two that we patrol every so often, but mostly the park rangers are in charge of security." Quinn's eyes gleamed, and Lucas figured his mind was tracking along the same lines as his.

"Let's get a list of the guests at the hotel and who had reservations at the campsites. Once we have that, do you have deputies who can go through that list and start going door to door?"

"I do."

Lucas turned to Kate who'd been listening with wide eyes. "Can you sketch the guy you saw?"

"I can draw what I saw—which unfortunately, wasn't much."

"That's okay. Anything will help."

She nodded. "I can do that before we leave. That will help get the picture out there faster. Especially, since there are technical issues still going on."

"How long will it take you?" Lucas asked.

"About ten or fifteen minutes."

Lucas raised a brow at the sheriff, who nodded. "I've got some pencils and paper around here somewhere. Let me check with Tris." He left and was back within a couple of minutes carrying a sketch pad and three freshly sharpened pencils. "Probably not the quality you're used to," he said to Kate, "but maybe they'll do?"

"They will."

She took them, sat at the sheriff's desk and went to work while Lucas pulled out his phone. "I'm going to make a few calls."

"That's fine."

Lucas stepped outside the office and dialed Tyson's number. The man answered on the first ring, and Lucas filled him in on everything, including Kate's efforts to sketch the guy. "She thinks it could be the same person in the car that ran us off the road our first night here. She said they had a similar build."

"Then he's been watching for you to come into town?"

"Looks like it."

"Okay, send me a copy of her sketch when she's finished. We'll keep it circulating. See if anyone recognizes him." He paused. "Do you want a couple of more team members out there? To keep an eye on things?"

Did he? Lucas seriously considered it. Then sighed. "Right now, I'm going to say no. If we have too many people around, it might just draw attention to her. Which she doesn't need. So, let's just leave things alone for the moment. Once we're back at the cabin, I think I can say with certainty that no one knows we're staying there."

"And you can get back there without being followed?"

"Yes."

More hesitation on Tyson's part. "Okay," he finally said, "but if you need backup, don't hesitate to ask for it."

"I promise I'll ask for help if we need it." They talked for another fifteen minutes about the case until finally Tyson said, "Keep an eye on the weather. Looks like it's supposed to get a bit nasty out there."

"Thanks, man. Tell the team I said hey and we'll talk soon."

He hung up and returned to find the sheriff studying the drawing over Kate's shoulder. She looked up with pleading eyes, and Lucas smothered a chuckle. Her annoyance was clear. He'd never seen that expression on her face before and found it cute. He cleared his throat. "You okay?"

"I'm fine. Just trying to get it perfect."

"Getting close?"

She nodded, swiped the pencil across the paper in a few more strokes, then held it up. "It was the best look I had of him."

Which wasn't much, but she'd done an incredible job of freezing the moment in time. "It was when I was looking out the window," she said, "and he glanced up at me with such hate in his eyes..." She swallowed. "He knows who I am. I shouldn't have called out and told you to hold him."

"It's okay." Lucas squeezed her shoulder in what he hoped felt like reassurance then rubbed his hands together and turned to the sheriff. "I'm going to check out my vehicle."

"Check it out?"

"Just give it a once over. I'm not sure it's a coincidence he swerved right into *my* SUV."

She nodded. "Okay. And if it's the same guy that attacked me at the rental, he'll have a goatee. Assuming he hasn't shaved it off."

"All right," Lucas said, "we're going to get out of here and head back up the mountain, where she can hide out once more. He might know we're around here, but he doesn't know exactly where, and just riding around looking for my car or hers—well, that's like looking for a needle in the haystack." He paused. "And now that we know he's around here, your deputies can keep their eyes peeled for him."

"Absolutely." The sheriff grimaced. "I'm sorry this happened. I'm sorry I had to have you come in, but it was the only expedient option. I'm just trying to catch this guy and wanted your input as soon as possible."

"We understand," Lucas said. "I think the guy is probably lying low for the moment, so we're going to take advantage while we can to make sure we're not followed."

"You want me to have someone hang back and watch your tail?"

Lucas hesitated. "How about they follow us to the edge of town and make sure no one is behind us? Once we're on the way up the mountain, I'll be able to keep an eye out and radio you if I spot someone."

"We can do that." Quinn grabbed his keys, and Lucas looked at Kate. "Stay here for just a few minutes while I check the car."

"Sure."

He walked out of the station and went to his vehicle, examining the area the man had hid.

He took off his gloves and ran his hands over the plate and under the edge of the bumper.

Nothing. He shook his head and nodded to the sheriff. "It's clean."

"Good." He walked to his cruiser and climbed in while Lucas went back to get Kate and walk her out of the station. He got her back into the vehicle without anyone stopping them.

But he had to admit, the hairs on the back of his neck were standing up. He let his gaze roam the area, and while nothing caught his attention, once he left the sheriff behind, he'd take a circuitous route back to the cabin.

Just to make sure.

FIVE

Once they were back at the cabin with Lucas's reassurances that no one had followed them, it didn't take Kate long to get a pot of chili simmering on the stove, filling her small side of the duplex with the tantalizing aroma of spices, sauce and meat. She also took the time to throw together a pound cake and get it in the oven.

Now that lunch was cooking, she found herself restless, the creative drive pushing her to get out and paint.

Yesterday, she'd found her favorite spot on the property. It was a wildflower meadow with a pond not too far in the distance. When the sun was high, it was warm enough for her to lose herself in her work.

Today was cooler and the skies a little darker, but still warm enough to enjoy the outdoors, so she'd set up one of the beach chairs she'd found in the closet, and while

Lucas and Angel trained, she sketched and tried to remember the night her life had turned upside down.

And to figure out who the person in the truck was. And why she thought she recognized the man from outside the sheriff's office. But the name and face eluded her.

While her thoughts spun, she swiped the pencil across the page then shaded an area on the man's face. Darkness invaded her and she wanted to quit, but she couldn't. Something inside her pushed her to keep going. Sometimes when she drew, she got so focused on the details, she didn't notice the full picture until she remembered to step back and take a look. For now, she wanted to get the man's jawline right.

She stopped and erased then penciled in a slight goatee. Yes, that was better.

Cocoa nudged her, and Kate scratched the little dog's ears. "I'm okay, girl."

Movement from the wooded area on the edge of the wildflower field caught her attention, and she stilled, watching, wondering if it was the wind or simply her imagination. She clipped Cocoa's leash on her collar then tied her to the chair. Cocoa hopped up into it and watched her with soulful dark eyes. "I'm just going to make sure everything's okay." She glanced around. Where was Lucas? He was usually somewhere close by, except when he needed to make a phone call as the best cell signal was inside connected to the Wi-Fi. He only used the satellite phone when he was out training Angel. Kate didn't see the dog, either. She picked up the rifle and took a few steps toward the woods to get a better look.

"Kate?"

She jumped then turned, heart pounding. "Lucas. You scared me."

"I was on the phone with my boss and saw you pick up the rifle. What's wrong?"

"I saw movement in the trees. I felt... watched. But I'm not sure if that's a legit feeling or if I'm just being paranoid because of... everything."

He frowned and pulled his weapon from the holster on his hip. "Stay here and I'll check it out." He turned his attention back to the phone. "Tyson, I'll call you back shortly." He hung up.

"It might be nothing," she said.

"Then we'll be grateful for that, but I'm still going to take a look." He glanced at Angel, who'd followed him out. "Angel, stay."

While Kate and the dogs looked on, he walked toward the woods, gun held in front of him.

Tension crept back into the base of Kate's neck and wound across her shoulders, tightening her muscles into bands of steel. When he disappeared into the tree line, she gripped the rifle and headed towards him. Cocoa barked, not liking being confined, but Kate didn't want the animal in danger should she decide to dart after whatever was in the woods.

Because something was there. She hadn't imagined it.

The trees swayed then stilled once more. Lucas came into sight, walking backwards, his weapon aimed at the woods. For several seconds, he stood there then slowly lowered the rifle. He turned and jogged over to her. "No two-legged creatures were there, but a mama bear and her three cubs were feasting on the blackberry bush a few feet in."

The breath she didn't realize she was holding left her in a rush. "Oh, wow. That's good news. I'm sad that I didn't get to see them." In her life before the attack, she wouldn't have been so hesitant to venture into the woods. She had plenty of experience around wild animals and knew how to act. But when she didn't know for sure it was an animal she'd be facing in the woods, caution had to rule. Still, her timidity sure was getting old. Her fingers spasmed into a fist. She'd never been afraid to follow her own path in life, but the events of the past few months had thrown her. Like they would anyone, of course, but it was time to stop being a victim and fight back.

Even though she had no idea what or who she'd be fighting.

"I think as long as we keep our distance," Lucas said, "and leave them alone, all will be fine. We'll need to keep the dogs nearby, too."

"Of course." She tilted her head at him. "I'm a wildlife artist, remember? I know how to handle myself. At least with animals. When it comes to humans who want me dead, I'm not nearly so confident." But she was trying.

"Understandable," he said, his voice low. He nodded to the sketch pad she'd set in the chair. "That's an interesting picture. Anyone I know?"

She frowned and looked down at her creation. Really looked.

And gasped.

"Kate? I was joking. What is it?"

She heard him say her name, but her mind was processing who'd she'd drawn.

"Kate?" He gripped her upper arm as though afraid she might keel over. She wasn't sure his fears weren't valid. "Talk to me."

"I drew him. I actually did it," she said, her

voice low. "I've tried before to draw what I saw that night and never did get it right. Seeing the man today sparked something. Maybe it was his eyes, I don't know. So, I decided to switch gears and just draw whatever came to mind, just doodling a mindless scribble while I thought about that night, but that's...him." She'd added the eyes to the blank face she saw in her dreams. Along with the goatee.

"The man from the night of the car fire?" Lucas's voice was sharp.

"Yes, but he's also the man from today." She looked up and swallowed. "I'm convinced more than ever that they're one and the same." She jabbed the picture with a forefinger. "*He's* the man who tried to kill me, and he's also the one you chased away from the vehicle. They're the same person."

The heat swept over her. Urgency propelled her. She needed to get out. Chloe! She couldn't see through the smoke as it swirled around her, choking her...killing her.

Move! *Her mind screamed the order, but her body couldn't obey. Her lungs spasmed, her mouth opened and her nose burned.*

"I can't breathe!"

She heard the shout, vaguely recognized that it came from her throat, but she was so buried in the memory she couldn't pull herself from it. Her fingers clutched the grass and pulled. *She was on the ground. She had to crawl away from the burning vehicle, but the baby, she couldn't leave her...*

Vaguely, she was aware of strong arms wrapped around her and her cheek snuggled against a hard chest. The cold button on Lucas's coat dug into her skin, bringing her back to the present. They were on the ground laying side by side, and he held her tight while he whispered something. She sucked in a wheezing breath, and finally his words registered. "It's okay, Kate. You're okay. Breathe. You're safe."

The words brought an instant rush of comfort. As did Cocoa's furry presence trying to get in between her and Lucas. The dog yipped, annoyed that she was being kept from her mistress. Then she flung her little body forward, her nose mashing into Kate's exposed cheek. "It's okay, Cocoa," she said. "I'm okay."

But the dog was having no part in moving. She licked Kate's face and tried to get up under her chin.

And Kate giggled.

Slowly, Lucas let her go, his gaze serious. She looked around, her mirth fading as fast as it had risen. "How did we get on the ground?"

"You dropped to your knees and I followed, catching you in case you were going to pass out. I was worried you'd hit your head."

"Oh."

"You okay?"

She swallowed, cuddling the little dog close, all giggles and smiles forgotten. "I think it's just the memories are coming back stronger and more often. There are some old memories mixed in there, but there are new ones, too. It was very odd. Like I was there—at the car fire. I could smell the smoke, feel the heat, but I also knew what was coming and that I needed to get away. Get to Chloe. But—" she pulled in a breath, a clean, cold, smoke-free filling of her lungs "—I knew she would be gone even if I could get to her. Memories…and more. Maybe some PTSD? I'm not sure."

"The 'getting the memories back' part is good, right?"

"Yes, of course, but it's almost debilitating." She glanced at her drawing again and shuddered. "And him. Putting a face to the shadowy figure I see in my dreams…well, it's unnerving." She frowned. "And I keep thinking I should know him. I should recognize who's trying to kill me, shouldn't I?"

"It'll come, Kate. I know you're ready to fill in all the blanks, and I know you're tired of people telling you not to push it."

"I am. Very tired of it."

"Then I'm not going to tell you that anymore. Come on," he said, rising to his feet and helping her to stand as well. "Let's go back inside and you can tell me about that night and what you remember once more. Maybe something else will shake loose."

"Okay." She set Cocoa on the ground, grabbed the sketch pad and closed it, not wanting to see the picture anymore.

He led the way back into the duplex, and she tossed the sketch pad onto the table then slumped onto the sofa. While Lucas made himself at home in the kitchen, Kate mentally ran through what she remembered.

Which was pretty much everything about that night. Almost. There were still some missing details, such as why Nikki had been so frantic that Kate take Chloe, but she was feeling much more confident those would come to her soon. The most important missing detail she just couldn't put her finger on was *why* someone wanted her dead. But they were going to have to figure that out before it was too late.

* * *

Lucas handed her the mug of hot chocolate then lit a match and got the fire going. Once the flames were dancing, he settled himself in the chair across from her. "I sent that drawing to Tyson. He's going to run it through facial recognition software and see if there's a hit. It's a long shot, but we both feel like it's worth a try."

She nodded. "You didn't have any trouble sending it?"

"No. Looks like the email glitches are on the sheriff's end, not ours."

"Good." She let out a low sigh. "It's nice to feel productive. Like I did something useful today."

"You did." He sipped his hot chocolate then leaned back in the chair. Angel settled beside him, and he dropped a hand over the armrest to run his fingers through her fur.

"Ever since this afternoon and seeing that man, I keep getting flashes," Kate said, "and I think I remember most of that night. There are a few gaps, but…those flashes come with more information attached to them."

"That's great."

She sighed. "Depends on your definition of *great* because I don't think it's enough to do any good—or help us find Chloe."

"Don't stress about it. Just start talking and let me listen."

"You sound like my therapist."

He studied her. "Has seeing him helped?"

"Some. I think. He's kind and definitely listens. He asks thoughtful questions and encourages me to take my time and not rush the memories, but…" She shrugged. "Other than that? I'm not sure. I like talking to him, I guess, or I wouldn't keep doing so." She paused and frowned. "Or maybe I keep talking to him in the hopes that I'll say something subconsciously. Like I'll remember something as I'm talking, say it and go, 'Ah, a memory! Finally.' But that hasn't happened yet. So far, the memories just seem to come when they want to."

"So, talk to me."

She drew in a deep breath and nodded. "All right. What do you want to know?"

"Tell me more about Chloe's mother, Nikki. Maybe that will help spark something else."

She sipped the hot chocolate then curled her hands around the mug. "Well, you know that Nikki and I were college roommates. We'd lost touch for a while after graduation, but when Nikki was six months pregnant, she called me and said she was moving back to Colorado."

"Did she say why?"

Kate nodded. "Because she was pregnant, not married and didn't know who the father was."

He winced. "That's rough."

"I wasn't sure I believed her, though. Nikki wasn't one to...do that. She was very pro-marriage and commitment. So to think she didn't know who the father was didn't make sense to me then and still doesn't."

"Did you ask her about it?"

"Yes. And she avoided answering me. Just said she'd made a mistake and didn't want to talk about it. I thought maybe she'd been assaulted, and it was just too painful to discuss, so I dropped the subject for the moment, hoping she'd open up at some point later on, but she didn't. And I didn't press. And now I may never know...um...sorry. Never mind."

Kate swiped a tear from her cheek, and Lucas couldn't help but want to pull her back into an embrace. While they were in the field and she'd had her moment of PTSD or whatever it had been, he'd held her, and once her terror had subsided, he'd been reluctant to let her go.

And that nearly sent him scurrying from the cabin. He had no intention of falling for the beautiful and mysterious Kate Montgomery. He couldn't offer her what she deserved, so he just needed to steel his heart and deal with it.

"Lucas?"

He blinked, pulled from his thoughts. "Yeah?"

"Where'd you go?"

Her soft question made him catch his breath, and he shook himself. "Sorry. I was thinking about something." He cleared his throat. "So, she called you out of the blue because she was pregnant. Why not before then?"

"I asked her about that, and she was kind of vague. But she'd moved back to Colorado, knew I was still living there and doing my art, so she called. We reconnected, and she eventually asked me to be her labor coach."

"What about her parents?"

"Her dad took off when she was a kid, and her mom died of cancer shortly before Nikki found out she was pregnant. So, I agreed to be there for her." A faint smile curved her lips and a sheen of tears appeared but didn't fall. "I was the first one to hold Chloe." She sniffed. "And Nikki named me as Chloe's guardian so that if anything ever happened to her—" She bit her lip and raked a hand over her eyes.

"You'd get custody?"

She nodded. "I was with her when she was born and because I work from home, I could keep her during the day while Nikki worked. I know one day I can get married and, in all likelihood, have my own biological children, but Chloe's special to me. She's the child I've never had. She's as much mine as if I'd carried her in my own body and given birth to her." She pressed her fingers to her trembling lips, and Lucas's heart clenched with compassion. "And," she said on a shaky breath, "it's killing me that I can't remember anything to help find her."

Cocoa hopped up from her spot in front of the fire and hurried to join Kate on the couch. She snuggled close then pulled back to lick her nose. Kate gave a small, choked laugh, and hugged the little mutt to her. Angel watched like an indulgent mama.

Lucas took in the cozy scene, and more of those feelings he really should ignore bubbled to the surface. He quickly squashed them. Hard. The fact that he was having to do that a lot was starting to worry him. "Listen to your therapist. Don't put so much pressure on yourself. Not that I don't understand the desperation you feel—" boy, did he ever understand "—but stressing yourself to the breaking point isn't going to find her, either. I think you have to find some balance."

She grimaced. "I know you're right. I just don't know how to do that."

"Take breaks. Try to remember, then stop.

If a memory seems like it's on the edge of your mind, then explore it. But if pushing it makes it fade, then stop."

She frowned at him. "Sounds like you have some experience in that."

He shot her a tight smile. "Not like what you're dealing with, but yeah, a little." And he wasn't ready to get into that.

Her clear desire for him to explain what he meant sent his pulse skittering once more. He didn't talk about his past to anyone. Ever. He stood and walked into the kitchen to stir the chili, thankful to have something to do while he dealt with his conflicting feelings. Her gaze followed him, and something flickered behind those hazel eyes. "You mentioned your wife leaving you," she said. "I know that was painful for you."

The statement froze him for a split second, then he nodded. "Everyone has some kind of pain. You can't go through life without it, unfortunately."

"Yes, but—"

"I've been thinking about how someone could have found you at the little rental you were in."

She snapped her lips shut, and he grimaced at his abrupt changed of topic, knowing he might have hurt her feelings. But he had to move on before her compassionate gaze undid him and he talked about things he'd worked hard to lock away into a little area in the corner of his mind. A place he never went to. But a little part of his mind wondered if maybe sharing with her, someone who hadn't known him all his life, would be therapeutic? She obviously found talking about her issues helpful.

But that was different.

How? the small voice in his head taunted him.

"And?" she asked.

Getting lost in tormenting thoughts around her was starting to become a habit. One he needed to break immediately.

"And I'm not sure. I talked to my boss yesterday about who knew you were at the rental house and he said just Skylar."

She nodded, and her hand curled into a fist. "Skylar found the house and escorted me there, but I don't know how she found it or what she told the person I was renting it from."

"Knowing Skylar, not a lot. She's big on privacy."

"Which I appreciate," Kate said.

He sighed and rubbed his eyes. "I feel like I should…confess something."

"Confess something?"

"I looked you up," he said.

She blinked. "What do you mean?"

He shrugged. "In the hospital, when I stopped by to see you on occasion, all I wanted was for you to wake up and tell your story. I didn't think about you as a woman with a…a…life. I mean, of course I knew you had a life, but…" He groaned. "I'm not wording this right."

She raised a brow and amusement flashed briefly in her gaze. "Okay."

He shook his head. "That sounds bad. And it was. When you were unconscious…in the coma, I would come by and talk to you. Ask you to wake up so you could tell me who had done that to you. But you just laid there, eyes closed." Looking so beautiful and helpless it turned him inside out every time he stopped by. "I was kicking myself for not being more intentional about learning who you were. So, not long before you woke up, I did a search on your name."

"Oh. Well, you didn't have to do a search. You could have just asked me."

He paused. "True."

"So, why didn't you?"

"Well, you were unconscious for most of the time. And by the time you were conscious, I was getting really busy and couldn't come by."

She glanced away then back. "Skylar told me you came to talk to me. That you'd stop in occasionally." She hesitated. "Every once in a while, you'll say something and it's like I've…heard you say it before."

"Really?"

"Yes."

He blinked. "Oh. Wow."

"I know. Weird, isn't it?"

He couldn't stop the flash of emotion that swept through him. "No, not at all." He cleared his throat. "So, why didn't you tell me you were famous?"

"Famous?" She laughed then shrugged. "I'm not really. Not like a celebrity in Hollywood or something. I can say that yes, in the art world, in that circle of people, I'm well-known."

"The sheriff knew who you were."

"Hm. Yes."

"So, you make a living with your art?"

"I do." She sighed. "I've been living on savings recently. Although I'm sure some of my other pieces from a gallery in Denver have sold and I have checks waiting on me whenever I can get there to pick them up—or let them know where to mail them."

"I can have someone take care of that for you if you need me to."

She raised a brow at him. "I might just let you do that. Thank you." She paused. "When, at the end of my sophomore year in college, I decided to change my major to art, my mother flipped. She was furious and told me that if I didn't stay the course and get my degree in business, she'd cut me off."

"Ouch. What?"

She nodded.

"And you went after the art, obviously."

"I did. Fortunately, my paternal grandparents left me some money on my twentieth birthday that my parents had no access to. It wasn't a lot, but it was enough to get me through the last two years of college, cover some monthly expenses and have a little left over. Now, I don't need the money, so I'm letting it sit there and earn interest while I build my business, market my brand, which is my name, and continue to chase my dreams. Painting and selling my art to people who find themselves drawn to it for whatever reasons. I have a friend who owns a gallery in Denver. She's very supportive of my work. People can order prints from my website and that order goes straight to the gallery, and they send the print off to the client. It's worked out really well."

"That's amazing."

She smiled, but it didn't reach her eyes. "If you looked up my name, then you probably know who my parents are."

"Brock and Violet Montgomery," he said. "Owners of one of the biggest shoe companies in the world, started two generations ago." In other words, lots of family money.

She nodded. "My parents had big plans for me. Like I said, when I didn't play nice, they cut me off. It was mostly my mother, I'm sure. I've spoken to them only a handful of times since everything blew up. Mostly around the holidays I'll call and we'll have a stilted conversation, and then all of us are relieved when we finally hang up."

This time it was his turn to blink. "Oh. I'm so sorry."

"I am, too," she sighed. "But lately, I was tired of it. The disconnect ate at me and I had planned to reach out to them, to see if we could reconcile, but then everything went haywire and I haven't wanted to bring them into this mess."

In other words, not hearing from their daughter for an extended period of time was the norm. How sad. "I can't imagine how lonely and painful the last months have been for you."

"It has been perfectly awful. Well, the months I've been conscious, anyway. As soon as I was able, I started working to get my life back, doing everything they said, pushing through the pain to do the therapy. Physical therapy, occupational therapy and mental health therapy. And, of course, there was physical pain even in the healing. So much pain, but if I don't find Chloe, that pain is nothing compared to losing her."

"I know," he said, frustration running through him that he couldn't *fix* things for her. It was disconcerting how close he felt to her—how comfortable he was with her. Like they'd known each other for years. He'd seen her in the hospital, of course, and she'd been a topic of conversation with the team since she'd been found and they'd gotten the case, but now, being with her, seeing her in person, talking to her, new feelings were growing with each passing moment.

And if he didn't get a handle on them, he was afraid this distraction might be the very thing that would get her killed.

SIX

Kate rubbed her eyes. She was tired but didn't want to sleep. Not yet. The nightmares might come, and she simply didn't have the energy to deal with them. Then again, if she didn't get some rest, she wouldn't have the energy for anything else, either.

Like figuring out who had taken Chloe.

Lucas served the chili while the flames danced in the fireplace. It was a cozy arrangement, but she didn't fool herself. Lucas was a handsome man, but he held himself aloof. Distant. He wasn't cold or rude toward her. On the contrary, he was one of the most kind and gentle men she'd ever met. But there was something about the way he held himself. The way his eyes never seemed to thaw completely.

It didn't take a genius to figure out that it was the pain in his past he carried with him every day.

She could relate. And talking about her parents had brought that pain to the surface. Pain she knew she needed to confront, deal with, put in the past and leave there should her parents not be open to resolving their issues.

When Lucas set his bowl on the end table and wiped his mouth, Kate leaned forward. "Will you tell me about her? Your wife?"

He stilled. Then was quiet so long she thought he was trying to figure out a way to say no.

"It's all right," she said, "you don't have to. I just don't want to talk about myself anymore."

He lifted his head. "I can understand that."

But it was clear he didn't want to talk about his ex. "Okay, different topic. Where'd you grow up?"

A smile curved his lips, and his eyes thawed a fraction. "In Idaho."

"What was your childhood like?"

He shrugged. "Normal, I guess you'd call it. My parents are middle-class and hard workers. My dad was a cop, and my mom was a nurse for years. She just retired last year, and so did my dad. They worked hard and planned it that way so they could be young enough to travel and enjoy their remaining years."

"How wonderful for them. And very smart."

He nodded.

"Any siblings?"

His gaze slid from hers, and he cleared his throat. "Ah, yeah. I had a sister. She died when she was eleven."

"Oh no! I'm so sorry. I shouldn't ask questions." She'd just wanted to take the focus off herself for a few moments, and now she'd made him remember something that pained him. Not that he'd forgotten, of course, but she'd brought it to the surface.

He shook his head and offered her a sad smile. "Honestly, Kate, it's okay. It's good to talk about her. To think about her. I worked very hard at not thinking about her after she died, so…" Another small shrug lifted one shoulder. "So, I guess what I'm saying is, don't feel bad."

"What's her name?" Kate asked, keeping her voice low.

"Crystal."

"That's beautiful."

He reached into his back pocket and pulled out his wallet then retrieved a small photo and passed it to her. "That's the last picture that was taken of her. I know most people keep photos on their phones, but I like having the paper to hold for some strange reason."

Kate examined the child in the picture sitting on the dock bundled in winter clothing, holding a fishing pole and grinning at the camera. "That's not strange." She smiled. "She looks like you."

He laughed. "She did. We had the same eyes, same color hair, same facial features. Hers were just smaller and softer. Feminine."

There was definitely nothing feminine about him. She handed him the picture. "What happened?"

"An accident. A stupid, avoidable accident."

"How awful. I'm so sorry."

He fell silent while he stuffed the picture back into his wallet. "We went camping two or three times a year. And when I say camping, I mean what people these days call 'glamping.' We had a nice RV with power, a television, everything. We used the same campsite most of the time, and it was a beautiful spot overlooking the lake where that picture was taken. We spent our days fishing and swimming in the summer, and ice fishing and skiing in the winter. This particular year was one of those winters where the weather did everything it wasn't supposed to do. It was unpredictable. Warm one day and freezing the next." His jaw tightened and his eyes flickered. "Crystal was eleven. I was fifteen. Mom and Dad rode into town because Dad wasn't feeling well. Mom's a nurse and suspected appendicitis. She told me to keep an eye on Crystal."

Kate's stomach dropped. She had a feeling she could predict where he was going with this story. "You don't have to tell me if you don't want to."

He shrugged. "I don't talk about it much." His gaze met hers. "Not as much as I probably should, but for some reason, I want to tell you."

But he didn't want to talk about his ex. Her throat clogged and her heart already ached with the pain of what was coming. "Okay."

"Crystal wanted to go down to the lake. I didn't. I told her maybe a little later, but she kept pushing me to go right then. I yelled at her to quit being a brat and climbed into my bunk to pout. Mom called not too long after then to say she was right and Dad was heading to emergency surgery. She wanted to know if Crystal was okay. I said she was fine. Mom said she'd update me later and hung up. I was kind of worried about my dad, but, to be honest, I was more upset about the fact that my girlfriend—who was supposed to be the love of my life—had broken up with me a week before we left for the trip. I begged my parents to let me stay home so I could try and patch things up with her, but they said the trip would be good for me, maybe give me a new perspective on things." He let out a low, humorous laugh. "I didn't want a new perspective."

"I can see that. You were young and in love."

"And selfish and stupid." He sighed and rubbed his eyes. "Anyway, at some point after the conversation with Mom, Crystal slipped out of the camper and I didn't notice she was gone until a little while later. In spite of my teenage issues, I did love my sister and was immediately concerned about her being outside alone. I went looking for her and couldn't find her. I was terrified because the weather had changed again and dropped to below freezing temps. I searched and searched, but nothing. After an hour of looking for her, I called the park ranger, who called the cops. Two days later, a search party found her."

She gasped. "Two days?"

He nodded. "That was the soonest they could get an S&R team out there. The dog found her almost an hour after they arrived. She'd frozen to death about a mile from the campground."

"In other words, if someone like you had been available, she might have been found alive."

"Yes. Don't get me wrong, there were teams even back then, of course, but in that remote location and with the weather the way it was..." He shrugged. "It just didn't happen like it should have."

"I'm so sorry," Kate whispered. Her throat tightened. "I'm so very sorry."

Tears shimmered in his eyes for a split second, and then they were gone. "I am, too." He cleared his throat. "Anyway, my Mom was never really the same after that, and my dad became something of a workaholic until it was time for them to retire. There was healing in time, but it took a while."

"Of course it did. Did they blame you?"

He sighed. "They said they didn't, but..." He tilted his head, his gaze unfocused as he pictured something only he could see. "They said she shouldn't have snuck out. They also said they should have taken her with them.

They said a lot of things." He shot her a sad smile. "I'm not sure what to believe on that front."

"They probably didn't…don't…blame you, but I can see you blame yourself."

"How can I not?"

"You were a kid."

He huffed and his eyes narrowed. "You don't have to make excuses for me, Kate. Yes, I was a kid, but I was old enough to be responsible for my sister. And I failed. I've vowed not to let that happen again if at all possible."

The anguish on his face broke her heart, and she went to him to kneel in front of him and place a hand on his. His fingers threaded through hers, and he closed his eyes. The silence between them wasn't awkward or uncomfortable. It just was. Finally, he opened his eyes. "Thank you."

"For what?"

"For letting me talk. It's been almost twenty years, and I need to be able to remember her. She deserves to be remembered."

"She's why you do what you do, why you chose this profession." It wasn't a question.

A small smile curved his lips even though the sadness still lingered in his gaze. "Yeah."

"Well, I for one am very grateful you do

what you do. I hate the way it came about, but you make a difference, Lucas. At least, you have in my life."

His throat clogged and he cleared it. "Thanks, Kate."

"I didn't know her, but I think she would be proud of you. And honored that you chose this way to remember her."

Some of the pain shifted at her statement, and he smiled. "Yeah, she would. She loved dogs and would have adored Angel. And everyone on the team would have loved her."

"Tell me about them. You never finished. I mean, I've met most of them, I think, but I don't really *know* them." She stood and returned to her seat on the couch.

"Okay. You might know all this."

"It doesn't matter. Tell me anyway."

"All right, let's see. I'll start with our boss. Sergeant Tyson Wilkes. I served with him in the Middle East. When he came home, he joined the Denver PD as a K-9 handler. When he and Echo, his dog, helped Special Agent in Charge Michael Bridges with the FBI on a high-profile case, the man was really impressed and asked Tyson to head up the team because of the great need is this area. And he recruited a lot of us from the time we knew each other in the Middle East. He's a good man. Has a lot of cheesy sayings, but there's no one who'll have your back like him."

"Sounds like a real friend. I hear he and Skylar set a date for their wedding."

"Yep. Then there's Nelson Rivers. He, too, is one of the former army rangers from the same unit Tyson and I were in."

"I remember hearing about him."

"He came from the Idaho State Police K-9 unit. He's our arson dog handler. Diesel can sniff out just about anything when it comes to arson detection. He's married to Mia, a woman he met while investigating your accident.

"Jodie Chen is the administrative assistant and keeps everything running smoothly. Well, running smoothly *now*."

"Now?"

"For a while, the unit was in danger of being shut down. It's a bit of a long story, but the brother of a former unit buddy had a grudge against Tyson and caused a lot of issues. He did his best to sabotage everything and get us shut down. Thankfully, Tyson and the rest of us figured it all out and managed to save the unit. We just got word that we're going to continue doing what we're doing."

"Oh my. You don't live a boring life, do you?"

He laughed. "No, that's one thing I can't complain about. I'm never bored." He cleared his throat. "You sure you want to me to keep going?"

"Absolutely."

"Okay. Let's see, Ben Sawyer is from the Wyoming State Police K-9 unit. He and Shadow, his dog, specialize in protection. He and his wife, Jamie, have a little one who's about six months old now. Chris Fuller is from the Phoenix K-9 Police Department. Turns out he and Ben are half-brothers. He's married to Lexie, who does tours in the Denver area."

"Ah, yes, I remember all of that." She smirked. "At least I can remember something."

He laughed. "Daniella Vargas was a part of the unit, but she decided to pursue a different career path when she met her fiancé, Sam." He looked amused at the thought.

"What kind of career path?"

"She decided she'd rather be a mother and wife to her soon-to-be stepson and husband." He shot her a slow smile. "She loved being a handler but said she has no regrets. The fact that she got to keep her dog, Zeus, was a bonus. She's completely content—or will be after their wedding in a couple of weeks."

"That's amazing."

"And then there's Reece Campbell. He's from the Denver K-9 Police. He's a good man. A good friend. He found out not too long ago that he's a father and I don't think I've ever seen him so happy. His dog, Maverick, is a German shepherd that specialized in crime scene detection. Next is Harlow Zane. She and her K-9, Nell, are a cadaver detection team. They're from the Santa Fe K-9 unit."

"That sounds like a tough job."

"Very, but it's necessary."

Kate shuddered. "And I'm grateful there are people called to do that kind of thing."

"Me too." He took a sip of his drink, shook his head then stood and grabbed his coat. "There are more, but I've been talking an awful lot. I think it's time I take the dogs out."

It didn't take a genius to know that was code for he was going to look around to make sure all was well. Because as cozy and comfortable as the last little while had been, she still had a killer after her.

Lucas wondered why he wasn't kicking himself for sharing so much personal stuff with Kate, but he wasn't. He should be, but he wasn't. And he had to admit, he felt... lighter. Maybe the lightest he'd felt since Crystal's death. It was possible that knowing how much Kate had gone through the past eight months—and how much she was still going through—made him feel like she wouldn't judge him. Whatever the reason, he couldn't take back the words now. Not that he wanted to.

He stood and pulled her to her feet then nodded to the window. "It's snowing, too. After I let the dogs out, I'll get some extra wood out of the shed in case we lose power."

"I'm going to call Skylar and check in with her."

"Sounds good. I'll be back in a few minutes." He shrugged into his heavy coat, threw on his hat and gloves then called the dogs. They bolted after him into the falling snow. It was covering the ground at a rapid rate, and soon poor Cocoa would disappear into the drifts. He'd have to come out and clear an area for her.

Cocoa finished her business and darted back to him, shivering. He picked her up and tucked her inside his coat to share his body heat with her. Angel, however, didn't appear to feel the cold at all and took her time to sniff every exposed area. "Come on, Angel. It's cold out here."

She perked her ears toward the tree line in the distance, and Lucas walked toward her, noting Cocoa had stopped shivering and fallen asleep against him. Angel barked and loped toward whatever had captured her attention. Lucas noted another set of tracks in the snow and whistled. "Angel! Come!" He used his serious, I'm-not-playing voice.

She skidded to a halt and spun to race back to him, plopping herself in front of him, waiting for the next order. "Hold on, girl." He scratched her head. "Heel."

She circled to his left side and fell into step with him. He followed the tracks until he found the two smaller sets and stopped. "That's a big ole grizzly, Angel-girl. And she's got two cubs. We don't want to mess with her."

Angel shook herself and edged closer to him while he scanned the area. He finally spotted one of the cubs halfway up the nearest tree. The cub was about a year old, and this was likely its first winter. Mama was probably getting them ready to den for the next five months or so, and he did not want to provoke the grizzly.

The snow fell harder, and he couldn't decide if that was a good thing or not. Hopefully, it would keep any would-be intruders out, but it also had the potential to keep him and Kate trapped in the cabin.

His satellite phone buzzed, and he pulled it out to see the number for the sheriff blinking at him. "Hey, Quinn. What's up?"

"Just thought I'd give you a little report on the hotel and RV name list we've been checking out."

"You find something?"

"Maybe. Looks like someone was camping out near the river just outside of town. It was the only site we couldn't match with a name."

"That might be our guy then."

"Maybe. He's gone now. The cold could have chased him off, or he could have gotten nervous after you almost caught him in town."

"Either way, he's not there now, huh?"

"Nope, but we're still keeping our eyes open."

"Okay, thank you."

Lucas hung up and went back to work.

While he gathered the wood, being careful not to press it against Cocoa still snoozing in his coat, he kept an eye on the surrounding area for the bears—and anything else that could be potentially dangerous. With Angel close by, his mind formulated a plan, mapping out an escape route. He had chains on the tires of his SUV and was used to driving in adverse weather, but he'd rather not have to do that with Kate. She needed a break from the drama her life had become. Then again, if that's what it took to keep her alive, then so be it. He had a feeling she wouldn't argue. Once again, his phone buzzed. Tyson. Lucas swiped the screen. "Hey."

"Hey, do you have time to have a team meeting sometime this afternoon?"

"Sure. What time?"

"Two hours from now?"

"I'll be online. The internet is pretty good up here, so it shouldn't be a problem. Otherwise, I can join in using the sat phone."

"Perfect. I'll send you the meeting link shortly."

Lucas made his way back to the cabin to find the connecting door open. He set Cocoa on the floor and the little dog ran into the other side of the duplex to jump at Kate. Kate picked her up and snuggled her close. "I just want to make a couple of phone calls then I can have some food ready whenever we get hungry."

"You can cook more than chili?"

Kate laughed. "Yes. I like to cook. It's therapeutic for me. A distraction. And believe me, I can use all the distractions I can get right now with a killer after me."

Lucas walked over to her and placed a hand on her arm. "We'll figure it out, Kate. We won't stop until we do."

Her eyes searched his for a brief moment before she sighed and nodded. "I know. Thank you."

"Go on and make your phone calls. I'm going to get my laptop set up for a business call."

She nodded, but the lines of worry etched between her brows didn't fade, and he hated that for her. He glanced at the clock then went to set up for the meeting.

Kate brought him a sub sandwich and some chips. "No cooking involved. Sorry."

"It's perfect, thanks."

"Okay, you do your meeting. I'm going to go…" She waved a hand. "Sit in front of the fire and think."

"I'll be done before too long."

She nodded and disappeared to her side of the duplex.

Lucas worked until time to log in. One by

one, the team members appeared on his screen. "Hey, everyone," Tyson said, "I won't keep you long, but wanted to say thank you for all you're doing out there in the field. A quick update on baby Chloe. We're still investigating all the different angles of the case, and with Lucas in Montana with Kate—who seems to be remembering more with each passing day—I really believe the missing pieces will soon fall into place. We're going to find her." Nods of agreement echoed his sentiment. "Now," he said, "we've all celebrated the fact that the unit is staying operational."

Cheers went up, and Tyson smiled. "But that means we've got our work cut out for us. We've got to make sure we keep our i's dotted and our t's crossed."

Snickers greeted his comment, and Lucas shook his head. Tyson never could resist a cheesy quote or saying.

"So, each one of you have turned in proposals for how to grow the unit and made suggestions on how to make it better. After SAC Bridges's initial review, he's asked me to take each topic and dig a little deeper. He also wants a list of resources that we believe we need to be even more effective."

Lucas stood and went to check on Kate.

She was asleep on the couch, her right arm thrown above her head. Cocoa lay at her feet and lifted her head when he peered in. Good. She needed to sleep. He checked the windows, looking for any movement outside and grimaced when he noted the snow falling once more.

He went back to his meeting, ready to jump in with his own thoughts about how to improve the team, while another part of his brain stayed alert to any noise outside the cabin that would indicate someone was there who shouldn't be. Because if it kept snowing, trapping them, and someone attacked, he and Kate were going to have to be able to take a stand and fight back.

SEVEN

When Kate had left Lucas on his side of the duplex, she'd planned to make her calls but had stretched out on the couch and fallen asleep instead. No surprise since she was still healing, and with the added stress of someone trying to kill her, sometimes her brain just hit a wall.

When she opened her eyes, she could hear Lucas still talking on the other side of the door. She yawned, sat up and reached for the landline phone. Even while she dialed Skylar's number, she still spun Lucas's story about his sister through her mind. It had broken her heart. Such a tragedy.

And yet, he'd taken something so horrific and turned it into something good. There was a verse she remembered from childhood: "As for you," she whispered, "you meant evil against me, but God meant it for good in order to bring about this present result, to keep many people alive."

No one had committed a crime against his sister, but Lucas could have become bitter and resentful, shouldered the blame and turned to alcohol or drugs to deal with his pain. Instead, he'd channeled the hurt into helping others—and he was definitely keeping many people alive thanks to his profession. Her respect for the man had been high to begin with, but now it was off the charts.

Her throat tightened, and she whispered a prayer of thanks to the Lord. He had placed so many good people in her path. From the first responders who'd kept her alive after the attack, to the hospital personnel and therapists who'd nursed her and given her life back to her. And to friends like Skylar and Lucas who were still fighting to keep her alive.

"Hello?"

Skylar's voice jerked her back into the present. "Oh, hi, Skylar. This is Kate."

"Kate! I'm so glad to hear from you. What's this number you're calling from?"

"The landline at the cabin. My cell phone doesn't always get a signal, and Lucas has the satellite phone with him." She paused. "Is this okay?"

"Yes. It says you're calling from South Carolina, I'm sure Lucas masked it. There's no way to trace it. How are you?"

"I'm okay for the moment. I'm settled in and just praying that I can stay hidden long enough for you all to find who's after me. Have you heard anything about Chloe and where she could be?"

"No, nothing. Unfortunately, I don't think we're going to find her without your help figuring out what happened that night."

"I was afraid of that. But the good news is I've remembered more."

"Really? Tell me."

The eagerness in the woman's voice almost made her smile. She filled her in on everything she'd told Lucas. Then groaned. "But I can't remember what happened after I drove to the meeting location. But, I must have met with Nikki because Chloe was in the car with me. The only thing I can think of is she was obviously in danger and wanted me to take Chloe to keep the baby safe. Only whatever plan we came up with didn't work, and now Chloe is in the hands of whoever killed Nikki and tried to kill me." Kate closed her eyes on the shaft of pain her words ignited.

"We're still looking into Nikki's background, but so far, we've come up pretty empty. She was a very private person."

"Yes, I can see that about her. She told me a lot, but I know she didn't tell me everything." Obviously, because she'd had no idea Nikki had been pregnant until she was six months along.

"She has some social media," Skylar said, "but didn't post much, and nothing that tells us who the father of the baby might be. We've tracked down all of her friends listed on her accounts, but none of them were much help as she really didn't keep in touch with them."

"I was her closest friend, so if she wasn't talking to me…"

"Right. What would really help would be if you remembered any little thing she could have said that would tell us who the father is. If we knew that, we'd have a whole new investigative direction."

A faint flicker of something lit up at the edges of her memory. Nikki and her laughing. Then Nikki placing Kate's hand on her belly so she could feel the baby kicking. Pictures on Nikki's phone.

"Kate?"

"I'm here. Just thinking. I'll keep trying to

remember. Maybe it will just hit me or something will trigger it."

"And then there's still the watch we found in Nikki's apartment with the initials 'S.M.' engraved on the back. We've never been able to link those initials to anyone in her life."

"Right. I'd never seen it before you showed me the picture of it. I know you found that in Nikki's apartment, but again, it just goes to show you that she kept her secrets." Even from her best friend.

"The watch was a very expensive one. You still have no idea who it could belong to?"

"No, I'm so sorry." But, again, something niggled at the back of her mind like she *should* have an idea. The flash of Nikki with her phone, showing Kate pictures once again tickled her memory, but as hard as she tried, she couldn't get her mind to reveal why.

"Okay," Skylar said. "I know you'll call if you remember anything else. On another note, Lucas sent us the picture of the man you drew from the night of the fire. It's nothing that we can really go on, but we're circulating it anyway asking if anyone recognizes who it could be."

"He could be anyone, Skylar."

"I know. But if someone was out there on

that road and saw him, they could have gotten a look at the car he left in. If we had a better description of that…"

"True."

"Not to mention the fact that it's likely he's working with a woman."

A beeping sounded in the background, and Skylar murmured something Kate didn't catch. "I've got to go, Kate. Stay in touch."

"I will."

She hung up and pondered her next move while Cocoa hopped up on the couch next to her and snuggled in for a nap. Angel looked at them from her spot in front of the fire, appearing to debate whether she wanted to join in, then settled her nose between her paws and closed her eyes.

Kate drew in a low breath while her nerves twitched. As much as she wanted to relax and convince herself she was safe, she simply couldn't do it. Someone had left her for dead, and once they realized she was still alive, had made it their mission to finish the job. Only by remembering could she bring this horrific situation to an end and get Chloe back.

Which brought her thoughts around to her therapist, Bryan Gold. She debated whether to call him or not. Knowing the phone number couldn't be traced was nice—not that she didn't trust Bryan to keep her location a secret—but she honestly didn't want anyone other than Skylar and Lucas knowing where she was. She dialed Bryan's number and waited, prepared to leave a message.

"Hello? This is Bryan."

"Oh, Bryan, hi. This is Kate."

"Kate!" His shout made her pull the phone from her ear. "Sorry, didn't mean to yell," he said, "I've just been worried about you and wondering where you were."

"I'm hiding out right now, lying low."

"I'd say so. I thought you may have dropped off the planet. Are you okay?"

"Physically, yes. I'm fine."

"Mentally? Emotionally?"

She grimaced even though he couldn't see her face. "That's a little harder to gauge. Better than I was a few months ago, not exactly where I want to be at the moment. But still hopeful I'll find Chloe and all of this will be over soon."

"Any updates on who's after you? Have you remembered anything?"

She told him the same thing she'd told Lucas and Skylar. "But I'm still stuck on some of the events of that night, Bryan. I just can't remember!" She let some of her frustration ring in her voice. This was Bryan—he could handle it. But the angst sparked a pulsing pain behind her right eye. She pressed cold fingers against the spot and concentrated.

"We've talked about this, Kate. You know that you can't push the memories. It's just going to cause you headaches. You'll remember when you're ready."

"I'm ready now," she muttered and closed her eyes.

"I know you think you are, but your subconscious could be protecting you from something." He hesitated then said, "Do you want me to come out to wherever you are? I know you said you're hiding, so if you'd rather not tell me, I'm fine with that, but just thought I'd offer."

"No, I can't say anything. Lucas is going to a lot of trouble to keep me safe, and while I trust you, I promised not to tell anyone where I was."

"Of course." Another two-second pause. "Who's Lucas?"

"A police officer with the Rocky Mountain K-9 Unit."

"You trust him?"

"Yes. Fully."

"Good. Then just stay safe. Relax, rest, read, paint. Do whatever you can to take your mind off everything, and before you know it, your memory will probably return when you least expect it."

"But that's not helping Chloe, Bryan. I need to remember now."

"But pushing it might keep those memories locked up longer. Listen to your therapist, Kate."

She groaned. "Okay. Fine. I'm listening. I'm going to go now and fix some dinner. I'll talk to you soon."

"Sounds good. Thank you for touching base. I was really worried about you."

"I know. I'm sorry. I won't wait so long in between calls from now on, I promise."

"I'll hold you to that. Goodbye, Kate."

They hung up, and Kate raked a hand over her short curls. She picked up the phone once more and stared at it. What if she were to die tonight? Would she have any regrets?

At least one.

She drew in a deep breath and forced herself to dial her father's number. She'd always gotten along better with him than with her mother—probably because they'd shared a lot of interests like skeet shooting and horse-

back riding. They'd both had an appreciation
for wild animals and loved to visit new places
and try local dishes. Her mother? She had
nothing in common with the woman, and if it
hadn't been for her father—and the fact that
she looked just like him—she'd have thought
she was adopted and no one had told her.

The phone rang once. Twice.

"Hello?"

Kate's throat closed.

"Hello? Who's there and how did you get
this number?"

"Hi, Dad."

Silence greeted her, and she almost hung
up.

"Kate? Is it really you?"

"You have someone else who calls you
Dad?" She closed her eyes at the joke that
slipped out. "Yes. It's me."

"Well. Hi. Ah…it's not Thanksgiving yet,
is it?"

"No, no. It's not." Could the conversation
get any more awkward? "I've had quite the
adventure and wanted to call and touch base
with you since…" *Since I'm not sure I'll live
much longer and didn't want to die without
reaching out.*

But she wasn't going to say that.

"Since?"

"I was in an accident, Dad."

"An accident?" The fact that she could hear the concern in his voice nearly undid her.

"Accident?" Her mother's voice reached her. "What accident? Who are you talking to?"

"Hold on, dear," her father said. "What do you mean, Kate?"

What did she mean? How much did she want to say? "I was… I almost… Well, I was in a coma for a couple of months, and I have some blank spots in my memory, but…"

"A coma? For a couple of months?"

He sounded stunned, and a niggle of hope began to grow. "Dad, I could have died and—" her throat tightened, but she was determined to say what was on her heart "—and I'm very thankful I didn't, of course, but I don't like the way things are between us. I don't want to die knowing you and Mother are angry with me." She finished the sentence on a whisper.

"Then come home." Her mother's alto voice filtered through the line.

"I can't right now, but…"

"Then we have nothing more to talk about." Click.

Kate gasped and choked back a sob. She clenched her teeth, refusing to let the tears fall. She'd tried.

And had been rejected once more. Seriously, everything always had to go as her mother dictated and nothing seemed to be likely to change that. Not even her daughter's brush with death.

Kate desperately needed a distraction and fixing dinner sounded like the best way to do that.

The door to Lucas's side of the duplex slammed into the wall, and she ran to the opening to see a snow-covered Lucas fighting the wind to get it shut again.

Once he did, he turned and yanked the hat off his head. "It looks like we're here for the duration."

"Snowed in?"

"Definitely heading in that direction."

She glanced at the lamp burning on the end table next to the couch. "Well, at least we still have power."

The lamp flickered and went dark.

Lucas laughed. He couldn't help it. "You never should have said that."

Her low groan reached him in the darkness,

and he snagged the flashlight from his belt and turned it on. The powerful beam lit up the room. And Kate. She'd planted her hands on her hips and pursed her lips. "Apparently not." Her words were dry, but she looked like she was fighting tears.

"Hey, it'll be okay."

"I know." She wiped a hand across her eyes. "I'm not upset about the power."

"Then what is it?"

"I had a conversation with my parents—" She waved a dismissing hand. "It's not important. I'll explain later. Right now, we need to figure out what we're going to do with no power." A low hum started, and she raised a brow. "A generator?"

He followed the sound to the refrigerator. "Well, at least the food won't spoil."

Angel pushed past her legs and joined him, sniffing his feet. He scratched her ears. "I can build a fire in both sides, and we can still use the stoves thanks to the gas. What do you want for dinner?"

"There's leftover chili and I can do grilled cheese sandwiches to go with it."

"You sure you don't mind cooking for me?"

"Of course not." She shot him an amused look, and his heart stumbled over its next beat. "I told you, I like cooking. I find it soothing. It de-stresses me."

He cleared his throat. "Then that would be great. Thanks." Even if it might not fill him up. But he vowed not to say a word and go to bed hungry if it meant seeing the stress of the last few months—and whatever else she was upset about—fade from her gaze. "While you do that, I'm going to brush out Angel. She needs it." He paused. "Or should I help you in the kitchen?"

"That kitchen is only big enough for one of us. I've got it. I'll let you know when it's ready."

"Okay, thanks."

She spun and headed for the kitchen on her side of the duplex with Cocoa on her heels. He breathed a small sigh of relief mixed with disappointment. She was right. That kitchen was small and helping would have put them in close quarters with one another. An arrangement he would not have minded at all. He shook his head. "Get it together, man. She's your assignment, not your girlfriend." And she wouldn't ever be. God had made it clear his job was to rescue people, not fall in love with them. His wife had been a prime example of that. Shana had been hiking with friends and gotten lost. When her parents had reported her missing, he and Angel had tracked her and the others down, and when she'd asked him out, he'd been intrigued enough to say yes.

He sighed. Shana wasn't a bad person, but she was too self-absorbed to make a good wife to anyone. But, blinded by her beauty, her smile, her praise, how she claimed she loved that he made her feel safe, he'd fallen like a rock in the water.

And while there was nothing wrong with any of those things in general, when added to her immaturity and her need to be the center of attention, it all added up to a big fat relationship disaster. Which he hadn't seen until it was too late. He'd been ashamed of course, but determined to make the marriage work. He'd scheduled a counseling session for them, and Shana had acted like he was asking her to give up their firstborn. That had been the day she'd walked out and filed for divorce.

He just had to try to remember that he'd done all he'd could and that both people in the relationship had to want to make it work. Placing the entire blame for his failed marriage on his own shoulders was foolish.

But…he hadn't been perfect, and he knew

there were things he should have done better. Like not take as many search and rescue jobs so he could be home more. That had been Shana's biggest complaint. His job. The very job that had brought them together. No, avoiding any romantic entanglements with anyone—especially anyone related to his job—was his best option.

He ignored his heart's protest, and he and Angel stepped out onto the deck off the back of the cabin. It was covered, but it was chilly. Angel would get a quick brushing then they were heading back inside. Darkness came early to this part of the world during this season. Normally, the floodlights would illuminate the area, but not tonight. Tonight, the moon cast a cold glow, bouncing off the fresh snow and making the whole area feel surreal. He grabbed the brush he'd left out there three days ago and patted his knee. "Come here, girl. Let's get this done." She did. "Sit."

Angel sat, eyeing the brush. Her tail swished in the snow and against the wood. She liked being brushed and quivered with excitement.

While he worked, he let his gaze roam the area. It was quiet so far. Eerily silent except for the sound of the brush whooshing through Angel's coat. His thoughts went to the case and the woman inside. Again. Why was it that every time he had a moment to think, he thought about her? "What do you think, Angel? I noticed you and Cocoa are starting to be good friends, too. Think we're in over our heads and need to run as far as we can before we do something dumb like get too attached?"

Angel's ears twitched at her name, but she didn't look at him. "I'm going to take that as a yes."

She barked once, and he laughed as he pulled the brush through her fur over and over. She wasn't shedding much at the moment, but he liked to stay in the habit of keeping her groomed.

It wasn't long until the smell of the food reached him. His stomach rumbled and he gave Angel a pat. "I think that's our cue. You ready to eat, too?"

Angel darted for the door, and Lucas rose to let her in, only to stop at the sound that came from the tree line. A sound that was very much out of place. His hand went to his weapon, and the hair on the back of his neck prickled. Someone was out there. Watching. And it wasn't a bear this time. He snapped his fingers to Angel, and she darted to his side. "Heel, girl."

She didn't have her working gear on, but she wouldn't stray from his side if he commanded her to stay with him. For a moment, he listened, his breath frosting in the night air. Lucas wanted to warn Kate to remain inside, but if he did, he'd lose whoever was in the woods. While he hadn't heard anything else, he still headed toward where he'd heard the sound, grateful he hadn't taken off his vest because he sure felt like a target at the moment. Finally, he reached the cover of the trees and breathed a little easier. No one had shot at him.

Yet.

His eyes had adjusted to the darkness, but it was still difficult to see, especially in the patches where the moon's light didn't reach.

A crunch of underbrush just ahead snagged his attention, and he shot forward toward the sound. "Federal agent! Stop!"

The footsteps picked up speed, and so did Lucas, pushing through the dense trees, trying to see, but not wanting to use a light and make himself a bullet magnet.

Frustration hummed through him. Just as he was about to give up, a whisper of a breeze to his left was his only warning. He went to the ground as something whooshed over his head. He rolled to see a man dressed in heavy winter clothing. Hat, scarf, gloves, goggles. That was the only observation he had time to register before the guy swung the limb he still clutched. This time Lucas wasn't fast enough, and the thick piece of wood caught him in the jaw.

He let out a cry of surprise, and pain flashed as his head snapped back. He went to his knees, fighting another kind of darkness. Before he could gather his wits, the attacker was running away, disappearing into the night. Angel whined and jumped at him. He ran his fingers over her head. "I'm okay, girl." He touched his jaw. No broken skin, but he was going to have a nice bruise. The sound of a motor reached him, and he didn't bother giving chase this time. The guy was gone, but Lucas had no doubt he'd be back. That was twice the thug had gotten the drop on him. It wasn't going to happen again. "Come on, girl," he told Angel. "Let's go check on Kate."

They made their way back to the duplex with Lucas on edge, hyperaware of every sound the trees and nature made. And he realized he should have been aware of the reason it was so quiet earlier. The guy had been close to the house. Watching from his spot near the trees. Disturbing the night animals and insects.

Lucas led Angel inside and locked the door behind them. He walked over to Kate's side of the duplex, noting she'd already set the table and was wiping her hands on a towel. Candles flickered in the darkness and the fire blazed in the hearth, giving the place a warm feel in spite of there being no power to run the heat.

"I was just getting ready to call you," she said without looking up. "Have a seat."

Lucas was hit by the homey feel of the moment. And how much he liked it. But the moment was overshadowed by the fact that someone had found them. She tossed the towel onto the counter then turned and met his gaze. And gasped. "Lucas, what happened to your face?"

"He was here. I chased him and he got the drop on me." Again.

Her face paled, and she gripped the back of the nearest chair. "How? How does he keep finding me?" Tears hovered on her lashes for a brief moment before she took a deep breath and blinked them back. She walked to the freezer and put several ice cubes into the towel from the counter then hurried back to him to press it ever so gently against his chin. He took it from her, and she clasped her hands together in front of her. "I mean it. How?"

"I don't know. I heard an engine so he must have had a car stashed near the road. I think he was here. Watching. When I took Angel out to brush her, he got nervous and tried to leave. That's when I heard him."

She nodded. "Okay, then I need to think. To decide what to do next."

"Yeah. Well, right now, what I want to do is eat. And think. We'll figure out the next step together, okay?"

"Okay," she whispered.

He hated the stress and worry that reflected in her gaze and on her face. He wanted to end this for her, but something was going on. Something he was missing. Something they were *all* missing. Whoever was after her had resources beyond the average criminal. But how was he going to figure out who?

He cleared his throat, relieved to see three sandwiches piled on his plate and a steaming mug of chili next to it. "I feel like I should have been in here helping." But if he'd been doing that, he never would have known about the man in the woods. And it was a good thing to know.

She'd filled the dog bowls, and Cocoa was already eating. Angel happily joined her.

"You were helping by letting me do it." Her eyes flickered, and she turned to snag two glasses of tea from the counter.

He walked over to take the drinks from her and set them on the table. She stilled and eyed him. "You okay? And I mean more than the bruise on your jaw."

"Yes, but I just wanted to reassure you that you're going to be okay, too."

She sighed. "I want to believe that, Lucas. I really do. But the truth is, if we don't find Chloe, then I don't know that I'll ever be okay again."

Lucas couldn't help it. He pulled her to him in a hug, and she rested her head against his chest. "We'll find her, Kate."

"I'm praying for it."

Lucas set her away from him, missing the feel of her in his arms in a way that said he was heading straight for trouble. He focused on the throbbing in his face and reminded himself once more she was an assignment. Getting personally involved was not a smart thing to do.

"Are you hungry?" she asked, moving to the place she'd set for herself.

"Starved. I can't tell you how glad I am to see three sandwiches."

She attempted to smile and it fell flat, but she waved him to the seat. "I figured you'd need more than one."

Once they were settled at the table, he waited while she said a short blessing then took a bite of the first sandwich. Then he rose and walked to the window to peer out. He could eat and watch the yard at the same time. After a minute, he asked, "How did you like being an only child?"

She shrugged. "Hated it."

He frowned. "I'm sorry."

"It's okay. Having Nikki was like having a sister sometimes. We just lived in different houses." She paused. "When I was in a coma, did anyone call my parents?"

"Yes, of course. Once we figured out your identity. But…"

"But?"

"They were out of the country when Tyson finally managed to track them down. I know he spoke to your mother."

She set her sandwich down and pressed her

fingers to her temples. "Okay. What about my father?"

"I don't know. He never said."

"I just spoke to my father, and he sounded genuinely stunned that I was in an accident and a coma." She drew in a deep breath and let it out slowly. "She didn't tell him."

Her voice was so low he had to strain to hear it.

"Surely, she did," Lucas said.

"No, she didn't." She looked at her plate, going still. Almost rigid.

"Kate?" When she glanced up, tears shimmered in her gaze. He reached across the table and grasped her fingers. "What is it?"

"It's just… I haven't talked to my parents in years. I guess it didn't occur to me that they—my mother—would know how close I came to death and…"

Didn't bother to come see her. Or pass the news on to her father.

Lucas wasn't sure what to say. He finished off two of the sandwiches before she cleared her throat. "To follow up on my answer to your question about how I liked being an only child, without Nikki, I don't know what I would have done."

"You didn't have other friends from school?"

He looked out the window once more and let his gaze scan as far as he could see. Which wasn't far. Was the guy out there? Would he be back tonight? He needed to call Tyson and request some reinforcements. But at the moment, he'd keep Kate talking as it seemed to distract her from her constant worry.

She shook her head. "I was homeschooled through graduation. Not because my parents thought that was best, but because it fit their image of what a good parent does for their child—and it enabled them to keep up with who I was exposed to, which honestly made for a very lonely childhood."

"*They* homeschooled you?"

"Oh no, not them. They didn't have time for all that would entail. They hired the best tutors." She paused. "I speak three languages, play four instruments and paint. I was to be a well-rounded individual."

"Looks like they succeeded in that."

"Hm. But their plan sort of backfired."

He raised a brow. "How?"

She blew out a low breath. "My parents are very wealthy—as I'm sure you've discovered." He nodded. "And they planned for me to take over the family business when they retired."

"The shoe business."

She smiled. "That's a simple way of putting it, but yes. They have stores in several countries. My great grandfather started it, and the CEO position has always been passed down to the oldest child. My mother is the current CEO and had originally planned to pass it down to me, her only living child, when she retires."

"*Had* planned?"

"Yes. I jumped ship, so to speak. Derailed her plans when I found art and fell in love with it."

"You're very good at it."

Heat crawled into her cheeks. "Thank you. My art tutor, Mrs. Greyson, was an amazing woman who encouraged me, praised me and made me feel good about the ability to create. She was a breath of fresh air in my otherwise stifling, privileged life. Not only that, she did something else for me."

"What's that?"

"She gave me someone to look up to. I adored her and wanted to be like her, so I watched everything she did. After years of listening to parents who criticized everything that didn't fit in with their idea of what should be, it didn't take long to figure out that I wanted to pattern my behavior after Mrs. Greyson's, not my parents'. She was always kind to others, never said anything negative. And if she did get mad—which wasn't often—she prayed."

"What did she get mad about?"

"Mostly my parents' treatment of me, I think. Don't get me wrong—they weren't physically abusive or anything, but I was their daughter when it suited their purposes, and I was expected to be invisible when it didn't." She shrugged. "She found me crying one night, and I wailed about how lonely I was. Even though Nikki and I saw each other at church on Sundays and occasionally got together for other things when Mrs. Greyson could make arrangements, it just wasn't enough."

"Make arrangements without your parents' knowledge?"

She nodded. "We had a lot of field trips. To art museums, concerts, the theater—anything that was considered appropriate for the upper class. Any time she could arrange that, Nikki always came. Her mother knew the situation as Nikki was very vocal about it. She even let Nikki skip school a lot to join us." She swiped a tear from her cheek, and Lucas clenched his fists. How could her parents treat her that way?

"Anyway, that night when Mrs. Greyson found me crying, she got this look in her eyes that said she knew exactly what I was feeling, then pulled me into a hug and said she wanted to introduce me to someone."

"Who?"

"God. She taught me how to pray and showed me that while I may be physically alone, I'm never alone if I believe in Him. I figured I didn't have anything to lose. And besides, she was so sure, so confident in Him that I... I don't know. It was almost like I didn't have a choice. I *wanted* what she had so bad." She smiled. "Best decision I ever made."

"She sounds like an amazing person. Where is she now?"

"She's still married and living in Denver with two grown children and three grand-children."

"How old were you when you started working with her?"

"Fourteen." Her gaze turned reflective. "She came at a time when I really needed her. I was starting to go down an emotional path that could have ended badly, but she managed to pull me out of a depression and showed me that no matter my current circumstances, if I was patient, things would change when I got older. And they did."

"But why would you being good at art keep you from being CEO of the family business?"

"Because I'd rather paint than sit in some stuffy office looking at the latest shoe designs."

He studied her. "That's probably the simplified version?"

"Yes."

She took the last bite of her chili and pushed the bowl away. She hadn't touched her sandwich. She caught him eyeing it and chuckled. "You can have it."

"You sure?"

"Talking about my parents always kills my appetite." She slid the plate toward him. "I can always fix another."

"You don't have to twist my arm. But I'm still confused about why your parents would completely cut you off."

"Because I went against their wishes."

He blinked. "Wow, that's cold."

"I know. Which is why I try not to think about it too much." She shivered, and he noted her efforts to suppress a yawn.

He put more wood on the fire then went to the closet and pulled out a propane heater. "You'll need this for tonight."

"Oh, thank you. I didn't know that was there."

"I let Skylar know we were without power, and she told me to check the closets." He rubbed his hands together. "Thank you for the food. And now, I'm going to…ah…slip over to my side and make some phone calls, take care of some paperwork. You get some rest, okay?"

She nodded. "You think he'll be back?"

"I don't know, but if he gets too close to the cabin, the dogs will let us know."

"Right."

"Holler if you need anything."

She lifted Cocoa from the floor and cuddled her under her chin. "I'm fine, Lucas. Thank you."

But the way she held the dog belied her confident words.

EIGHT

Kate lay in bed, staring at the ceiling and fighting sleep. She'd been found. *They* had been found. Sleeping didn't seem to be an option at the moment, but she knew Lucas was right. If anyone got too close to the cabin, the dogs would sound the alert.

But now she was back to being afraid of the nightmares she knew would come, and while they were usually intermittent, she'd had a few since waking to find someone in her bedroom trying to kill her—along with everything else.

Understandable, of course, but not something she was eager to revisit. Cocoa raised her head then walked over to give Kate's nose a swipe with her tiny tongue. Kate pulled the animal to her chest and let out a sigh.

Lord, please help them find who's doing this. Thank you for keeping me alive through the crash. Thank you for the hope that Chloe's still alive and being taken care of. Please let me get her back so I can raise her to know her mother. A mother who loved her so much...

She finally drifted into sleep, and just like she'd feared, the nightmares came. The kind where she knew she was dreaming and ordered herself to wake up. But couldn't.

This time she was at Nikki's house with Chloe on her lap. Nikki was sitting beside her, showing her pictures on her phone, swiping too fast for Kate to make out what the pictures were. "Nikki, stop."

But Nikki wasn't there anymore, but Kate was on the road to meet her. Time had passed in the blink of an eye.

"Please, Kate, I need your help," Nikki's pleas had tugged at her, and she'd gone. The feelings from that time were real and just as terrifying because she knew what was coming and could do nothing to stop it.

Wake up! Wake up!

And still she drove, heading toward danger. The hair on the back of her neck rose. This time, something was different.

But...what?

She pulled to a stop in the wide-open area and got out, looking around the designated meeting spot Nikki had chosen and texted her directions to. "I have to be careful," her friend had said, her voice shaky and scared. "I have to make sure he doesn't follow me."

"Who?"

"I'll tell you everything when I see you. Just meet me there, okay? Please, Kate! I have to leave now before he comes back!"

"Okay, okay. I'll be there."

The dream shifted. She was back in the car with baby Chloe strapped safely in the back, her favorite stuffed pink rabbit clutched in her fingers. The baby babbled, and Kate's fingers flexed around the wheel. "It's going to be fine, sweetheart. Everything's going to be fine." Saying the words out loud was supposed to help. It didn't. What had Nikki gotten her mixed up in? Who was she so afraid would "come back" that she had to run? Headlights bounced off the rearview mirror, and she squinted. Was that Nikki following her?

Or…someone else?

Or it was no one and Nikki's paranoia had rubbed off on Kate. She pressed the gas. The headlights drew closer. It was him. The man with the hoodie.

And the crash was coming.

But wait. She hadn't seen Nikki yet! Chloe's

cries reached her. When had she put the baby in the back? She was so confused!

Wake up! Wake up!

The impact was followed by unbearable heat, a smothering sensation, choking, clawing to get of the car, crying out for Chloe. She made it out of the vehicle, away from the flames, head throbbing, the pain blinding. The man in the hoodie walked toward her. She wanted to scream, but the blackness sucked her under.

Kate thrashed, the sheets tangling around her. She wanted the dream to end...and yet, she didn't. Deep down, she knew she might remember something if she let the dream play out.

"If I need to hide out somewhere, I want to go to Montana," she'd told Skylar.

The woman frowned at her. "Why?"

"I don't know. I just need to."

Still looking unsure, Skylar nodded. "All right, give me a little time to make it happen."

Then she was in the little rental house, just before Lucas came to rescue her.

A hard hand clamped over her mouth.

More suffocating.

She needed to *breathe*!

Kate jerked upright with a short cry, her

heart pounding, gasping in gulps of air. Once she got her pulse under control, she flopped back onto the pillow.

Cocoa whined at the door, and Kate glanced at the clock on the nightstand. It was still early, but the sun would be coming up any moment. "All right, girl. Let me get dressed, and we'll go out. Very quickly." Once she was ready, she grabbed the rifle and cracked open the door. Then hesitated. Someone had been watching last night. Someone knew where they were. If she went outside…

Cocoa slipped through the crack and darted out.

Right into the snow that had piled up next to the door. "Cocoa! Wait!"

But the pup pushed through and came out on the other side of the light, fluffy, beautiful powder. The kind of snow kids pray for so they can spend the day in it.

The sun was rising, filtering through the clouds and allowing her to see a few feet in front of her, but that was about it. "Whoa." Cocoa didn't seem to mind it at all, plowing a path through the soft flakes, more inclined to play than to take care of business. And Kate didn't want to be outside. Not after what happened to Lucas last night. But she had the rifle, and Lucas was just inside. Then again, if someone decided to use her for target practice…

"Come on, Cocoa. It's freezing out here." The dog ignored her and trotted toward the woodshed. "Cocoa…"

She pulled her coat tighter under her chin and walked forward, tucking the butt of the rifle under her arm and keeping her finger near the trigger. She watched Cocoa finally find her spot. A gust of wind whipped Kate's hair around her face hard enough to sting. She shoved it away with a gloved hand, her heart pounding a little faster, wanting to get back inside. The little dog stopped, swiveled her head toward the shed and barked.

Kate stilled. "Cocoa, come!" Cocoa stopped barking and ran back toward Kate then turned back to the shed.

"Kate?" Lucas called to her from his open door and her heart settled. "You okay?"

"Yes, just letting Cocoa out. I'll be there in just a second."

He nodded, his gaze running over the area. "Come on back inside. I don't like you being out there."

She didn't like it, either. "I'm coming. Come, Cocoa!"

"I'm going to grab my sweater," he said, "then I'll take Angel out."

"Okay."

He backed inside, leaving the door cracked.

Cocoa ran toward the shed, and Kate stomped her foot and started to chase after her then stopped. "Cocoa, come now. Let's get a treat." The little dog finally spun and ran back toward Kate. Kate bent to scoop her into her arms and turned to head back toward the cabin, but Cocoa wiggled to get down and barked several times.

At the crunch of a step in the snow behind her, fear swirled in her chest.

She spun. A hard object grazed the side of her skull sending a lightning bolt of pain through her head.

She screamed and fell to the ground, Cocoa tumbling from her arms, the rifle falling from her hand while blackness threatened to sweep over her.

Lucas pulled the sweater over his head just as the scream sounded from outside the cabin. It froze him for a millisecond, but when Angel jumped to her feet and barked, Lucas grabbed his weapon and dashed for the door. "Kate!" He scanned the snow-covered landscape and spotted the tracks leading to the woodshed. "Kate! Where are you?"

Cocoa's high-pitched bark mingled with the roar of an engine. The noise pulled Lucas alongside the trail of footprints and around the corner of the woodshed to find Kate pushing herself up off the ground, blood dripping from a wound on the side of her forehead. "Kate!" He rushed to her and dropped to his knees beside her, gaze searching the area. "What happened?"

She raised a hand to her head and groaned. "I got ambushed." She huffed a short laugh. "Great. The last thing I need is another concussion."

"Come on, let's get you inside so I can take a look at that. I called Skylar and Tyson last night and let them know someone's found you. It's just a matter of figuring out where to go from here. And it looks like we need to fast-forward the timeline and get out of here."

"But how did someone find me? Skylar's the only person who knows where I am. I didn't even tell my therapist."

He shook his head. "I don't know." He shifted so he could help her to her feet. "Whoever whacked you had transportation nearby. Considering the depth of the snow, it was probably a snowmobile." That explained the sound of the engine.

She swayed, and Lucas kept a tight grip on her bicep. "I'm just about done," she said, her voice low. "I can't keep doing this forev—" A gasp slipped from her, and she pulled out of his hold to drop back to her knees.

"Kate?"

She didn't answer. She reached out a shaking hand and picked up an item from the snow.

"Kate, what is it?"

"This." He lowered himself beside her once more so he could see her face and the object she held. Now, he could tell it was a stuffed animal. A pink bunny wearing a little pink dress and a bonnet. She lifted the toy to show him. "It's Chloe's," she whispered.

"What?"

She touched the scuffed nose then traced the tattered ear. "I gave it to her when she was born. Eleven months ago. She had it with her the night of the accident." She paused. "Although, why I keep calling it an accident, I don't know. It was deliberate. Someone ran me off the road and attacked me and set my car on fire and stole Chloe!" The rage in her words shimmered between them. She wasn't hysterical—she was furious. He didn't blame her.

The chill that swept over Lucas had nothing to do with the weather. He placed a hand on hers, careful not to touch the bunny. "This is evidence. I need to bag it. I know you have gloves on, but try not to touch it anywhere else." He lifted her chin to raise her eyes to his. "Did you hear me? You okay?"

She nodded. "I'm okay. And I hear you." A piece of paper fluttered out from under the little dress and landed next to her knee. She snatched it by the edge and unfolded it.

His eyes landed on the typed words.

Stop searching for Chloe or she dies.

Kate let out a small cry and let the note flutter from her fingers. "Lucas, she's alive!" She scrambled to her feet, her head wound seemingly forgotten. She gripped his wrist. "She's still alive. This proves it. And she's still out there waiting for me to find her."

Tears tracked her cheeks, hopeful tears this time, and Lucas pulled her to him, careful not to hurt her head, while he considered this new development. "All right, this changes things."

"How?"

He pointed to the bunny. "Angel has something to track the guy with. This is a search and rescue mission now. My partner and I have got work to do. Come on."

He helped her to the house, calling for the dogs to follow. They'd run off their energy and were covered in snow that would melt all over the floor, but that was the least of his worries. He settled Kate into the recliner in front of the fireplace on her side of the duplex, and Cocoa jumped in her lap to lick her face while Angel watched from the spot she'd claimed on the floor.

Lucas dialed Tyson's number and grabbed a washcloth from the bathroom while the phone rang. He returned to kneel in front of her and pressed the rag to her head. She used one hand to help. "You said 'search and rescue mission.' You're going after her, aren't you?"

"If I can." When the call went to voice-mail, he left Tyson a message to call him then took her free hand in his. "I know it's hard, Kate, but you can't give up. You have to keep fighting."

She closed her eyes and frowned while she held the cloth against her wound. "I know. More than ever now, of course. I just don't understand how this person seems to be able to find me no matter where I go or what I do."

Her despair, mixed with the hope of receiving what she took as confirmation that Chloe was alive, reached out to wrap itself around his heart. A heart he was having a harder and harder time steeling against this attractive, vulnerable woman. His argument against getting involved with anyone he rescued or worked with was starting to fade into the background. "I know. I don't either. I keep going back to the guy on the bicycle. I'll check my vehicle again for a device, but first, let me see to your head." He headed for the bathroom while his thoughts spun. He needed to get Angel and get her on the scent, but he couldn't leave Kate hurt and alone.

He'd spent the night listening to her toss and turn on the other side of the duplex, obviously troubled by nightmares. It had been all he could do not to offer her comfort, but he'd stayed put and let her battle her dreams by herself, praying that by doing so, she'd wake up with another memory intact.

Later, when he'd figured she was awake, he'd walked to the door to knock, and heard her low voice and realized she was on the phone. No doubt seeking comfort from either Skylar or her therapist. It hurt that she hadn't come to him.

Stop it, Lucas. Just stop.

He grimaced and grabbed the first aid kit from the linen closet. Why get his heart involved when it would just get broken when the case was over and she returned to her former life? Assuming she lived to do so.

The thought had him clenching his fists and pulling in calming breaths before venturing back into the den. She would live. He'd see to it one way or another. Kate held the cloth to her head, and her eyes were closed. He knelt beside her once more, and she turned her head to look at him. "I'm sorry I'm so much trouble."

"It's not you, Kate. You know that."

She sighed. "Thank you. Yes, I do know. I suppose it was really stupid of me to venture out by myself, not that I planned to, but Cocoa slipped out the door and the thought of losing her…" Her jaw tightened, but it was the flare of raw fury in her gaze that paused him.

"That's it," he said.

"What?"

"That anger. Use it. Channel it into the energy to keep fighting."

She left her eyes locked on his for a moment longer, and the urge to protect her nearly knocked him sideways. But she gave a faint nod, and he focused his attention back on her head. It didn't take him long to clean the area and bandage the cut. "I think it was a glancing blow," he told her. "I'm sure it hurt, and you're probably going to have a headache, but it definitely could have been a lot worse."

"I heard him and turned just as he was swinging." She paused. "What did he hit me with anyway?"

"A piece of wood from the shed."

Lucas's phone rang and he glanced at the screen. "That's Tyson. I'm going to fill him in on everything. I'll be right back." He dug two little orange pills from the box and pressed them into her hand. "For the headache."

She took them without hesitation, and he swiped the screen on his phone. "Thanks for calling me back so fast," he said by way of a greeting.

"Of course. What's the latest?"

Lucas filled him in while he gathered the things he'd need for Angel. "He's out there somewhere, Tyson. I want to take Angel and see if she can track whoever left the bunny and the note, but I hate to leave Kate here alone. She's got a head wound. And by the time we get someone out there to stay with Kate, Angel might not be able to pick up the trail." The longer he waited, the more the snow would cover any tracks. The clock was ticking.

"You need to try, Lucas. Here's what we'll do. I'll call local law enforcement to ride over there."

"I'm not sure they'll be able to get through. The snow is pretty deep and still coming down. The guy was on foot, but I heard an engine so I'm guessing he probably has something with chains on it or a snowmobile."

"The deputies should have snowmobiles, too. They know what to do in this kind of weather. All we can do is try, but you need to go after Chloe. This is a huge lead and might be the only chance we've got to find her. I'll do my best to get some reinforcements out there, but it's going to take a while—especially in this weather."

"Yeah. You're right." Kate would understand. In fact, she'd insist on him going. "Angel and I are headed out ASAP."

"Good. Be careful and keep me informed."

"Will do."

He returned to Kate's side and told her what he had planned.

Her eyes widened. "I want to go."

"Not this time. We're going to be moving fast and you're injured." The thought of leaving her alone still bothered him greatly, though. What if the person who'd attacked

her circled back? If that was the case, Lucas
would be on his tail. "Please promise me
you'll lock up and stay put. Keep the rifle
and Cocoa close by. The longer I wait to go
after him, the colder the trail gets." Literally.

She bit her lip and nodded. "All right. Go."

He took the paper bag he'd placed the
bunny in and called Angel over. His partner
hopped to her feet, tail beating the air. Excitement rippled through her. She was ready.

Lucas slipped the harness on her and
clipped the leash to it then looked at Kate.
"We'll be back."

She nodded, hope in her eyes. He could
only pray he could live up to it. He hadn't
been able to save his sister, but this time
would be different. *Please, God, I know I've
been angry with You, but this is Kate and a
little baby. Please let this time be different
and help me find Chloe.*

He glanced at his SUV parked next to the
lean-to and noticed it looked odd. He hurried
over to it and swept the piling snow from the
back tire.

Slashed. "Oh man. You've got to be kidding me," he muttered.

He checked the other tires and found them
in the same condition. Angel looked up at

him, her expression a mixture of eagerness and impatience. "All right, girl. Guess I'll have to deal with this after we catch the perp." He took Angel to the place where Kate had found the bunny and held the open bag out to the dog. The border collie sniffed it. "Angel, seek. Find Chloe."

Angel removed her nose from the bag and lifted it to the air, snout quivering. She barked once and spun toward the trees indicating she'd picked up the scent. Adrenaline surged. "Good girl, Angel. Good girl."

She darted ahead of him, legs kicking up the snow. Lucas pounded as fast as he could behind her, but the snow was deep and made for slower going than he would have liked. Angel changed directions slightly and headed down the mountain. Lucas could still see the tracks made by Kate's attacker. The snow was filling them in fast, but they were still there. For the moment. Which meant Angel was heading in the right direction.

For about half a mile, they jogged, and Lucas's hopes were high. Through the trees, he spotted something metallic. The sun winked off of it, and Lucas frowned. "Come on, girl. Let's go see what that is." He and Angel picked up the pace once more. He slowed when they got closer and held his weapon ready, suspicious that it could be a trap.

A snowmobile sat empty and powered down on the side of the path. And fresh footsteps led away from it. "Think that's our guy, Angel. And I'm guessing he didn't check his gas gauge before he decided to do his dirty work."

With his nerves on high alert and ears searching for any sound not associated with the wooded area, Lucas followed the footprints, Angel slightly ahead. When he and Angel came out of the trees to a rugged two-lane road, Angel stopped, sniffed, then whined while she paced, looking for the scent she'd lost. Lucas wanted to whine with her. Finally, she sat next to the fresh snowmobile tracks, still faintly visible beneath the freshly fallen snow. Lucas bit back a low groan. They were too late. Whoever had abandoned the snowmobile had called someone to meet him. There were definitely two people involved in this. But who? Who stood to gain if Kate was dead?

NINE

Kate pressed a hand to her aching head and stared out the window. With Lucas and Angel on the heels of her attacker—and, hopefully, uncovering Chloe's location—all she could do was wait and pray. She glanced at the phone and considered calling her therapist again, but for what purpose? She'd just talked to him and had nothing more to report. Then again, it might be nice to hear him tell her that all was going to be all right.

She turned to the end table and reached for the cordless handset only to remember she had no power. And Lucas had the satellite phone with him. Which meant she had no way to call anyone. She curled her fingers into a fist. She needed to stop relying on Bryan to boost her morale. The more she thought about it, the more she realized he simply said the same things over and over.

Nothing bad, of course. He talked about things that were comforting and absolutely true, but she needed more than that. She needed more than answers that were starting to feel patronizing. She needed—wanted?—Lucas. And she wasn't even sure how or when that had happened, but it had, and now she had to figure out what to do about that.

Which was nothing. For now. Her feelings could be all mixed up and tied in with having him ride to her rescue, his determination to keep her safe, his encouragement and admiration that sent her self-esteem skyrocketing. And it wasn't like she was desperate for those things or had never had a man admire her before. But with Lucas, it was different.

She sighed. What she *probably* needed to do was stop overthinking things, listen to her therapist, believe his assurances that she'd remember when she was ready and stop stressing about it. But…how was she supposed to do that when Chloe was still out there? She bit her lip on the tears that wanted to rise and fall and let the memories from Chloe's birth wash over her. From seeing her for the first time, to holding her, feeding her, singing to her when she was restless and wouldn't sleep. They were such precious times. Times she wasn't ready to have end. "I'm not giving up, baby girl," she said. "I'm going to find you no matter how long it takes."

Cocoa walked over and stood on her hind legs, front paws braced on Kate's knee. Kate picked up the mutt and kissed her head. "You've been a real lifesaver, little one. You always make me feel better." Nothing could completely take away the pain of losing and missing Chloe, of course, but the dog's presence did comfort her greatly.

A knock on the door sent her heart pounding, and she set Cocoa on the floor then gripped the rifle with both hands. "Who's there?"

"Kate? It's me. Don't shoot."

She hurried to the door and unlocked it. Lucas and Angel stepped inside, snow blowing in around them. She shut the door and leaned the rifle against the wall then eyed him, desperate to hear what he found. "Well?"

"I'm sorry, Kate. We tracked him to where he got with his snowmobile. I had no way to follow."

Despair swept over her, and she pressed cold fingers to her lips to hold back the sobs that wanted to escape. After several deep breaths, she nodded. "Thank you for trying."

"Hey—" He pulled off his gloves and set them on the end table next to the sofa, shrugged out of his coat then turned back to her and gripped her biceps in a gentle hold. His touch calmed her and sent her pulse racing all at the same time. She stood still, waiting for him to continue. "—we're not giving up. This is a huge step in the right direction. The person who has Chloe messed up."

"I'm not giving up. I just need to process the disappointment and move forward."

He nodded. "Okay, then. Good."

"What do you mean, 'messed up'?"

"They left behind evidence for one. Second, they let us know we're definitely on the right track and closing in on finding her. And third, we've got them worried."

"Right. True. That's good."

He studied her for a long moment, and Kate stepped forward to rest her head against his chest. His heart beat beneath her cheek, and his arms came up around her.

"Thank you," she whispered. "I honestly don't know what I would do without you."

His arms tightened, and she thought he might have kissed the top of her head before he cleared his throat and stepped back. Embarrassed that she might have made him uncomfortable with her words and actions, she wrapped her arms around her waist and focused on the main question. "How did someone find me, Lucas? We were so careful. The only person who knows where I am is Skylar."

"And the two deputies who followed us out here," he said.

"And the sheriff and Tris, the desk sergeant. But surely none of them would be involved in this. My coming here was so random and basically unplanned that I just don't see how this person is staying right on my trail. I didn't even tell my therapist where we were. I mean, I called him, but the number is routed to disguise the location, right?"

"Yes. I don't see how anyone could have traced the phone. One thought that comes to mind is my vehicle. It's low-key with the logos on the side, but it's still recognizable as a law enforcement vehicle."

"You think they followed us from town?"

"Maybe. I was watching very close and never noticed, but that doesn't mean…" He sighed, stepped back and raked a hand through his hair. "I'm sorry, Kate. If I somehow led them to you, then…"

"It's not your fault." She paced to the window and looked out. The peaceful view was at odds with the angst rolling through her.

"The sheriff's car was parked right next to mine," Lucas said.

She turned. "Yes."

"When the guy bumped into my SUV, it's very possible he planned to put a tracker on it. But then, when he realized he was spotted, switched up his plan and put it on the sheriff's car." He pulled out his phone. "I'll get him to check."

"Why put it on his car?"

"It was probably a long shot, but maybe since we'd had an escort before, he figured we'd do it again?" He held up a finger for her hang on a second and explained to the sheriff what he was thinking. "Yes, I'll hold while you look."

Kate twisted her fingers together and Cocoa came to her. She ran her hands through the silky fur.

"Okay, thanks," Lucas said. He hung up and nodded. "The sheriff found it under his license plate."

"Wow. But the sheriff didn't follow us all the way here, just long enough to ensure that no one was behind us."

"He didn't have to. Once we were on the

road here, it's pretty much a straight shot. All the guy had to do was drive around until he found the right area. And our cars aren't exactly hidden." Because there was nowhere to hide them. "Needless to say, he knows where you are."

"So, do I run again?"

"Where would you go?"

She shook her head. "My parents?"

"I don't think that would be wise. They may have someone watching them to see if you show up. Besides, I didn't think you were on speaking terms with them."

"I'm not sure how I would define the terms we're on, but my father sent me an email. I read it on my phone this morning. He said he tried to call, but couldn't get through."

He raised a brow. "What did he say?"

She shrugged and summarized. "My mother never told my father that I almost died. He was truly shocked. He talked to my mother about it, but I'm not sure anything's changed. I *do* think my father loves me and has missed me, but he's not willing to stand up to my mother about that fact due to some history there—" like not wanting to upset her mother or risk his money flow being cut off "—so, I don't know. He asked me to come stay with them. Their house is a fortress with tons of security, but I said no." Maybe she was being too judgmental and harsh, but it hurt. It hurt so much that he would be so influenced by such a thing. She sucked in a breath. "And, with the snow coming down like it is, I'm not sure I could go anywhere if I decided to anyway. If Chloe's in the area, I don't really want to leave." She picked up the bag with the stuffed bunny in it. "Not when we're getting so close. At least, I believe we are."

He joined her at the window. "I think we are, too, and like I said, that fact has got someone real worried." He shook his head studying the weather. The frown on his face and the look in his eyes shook her.

"What is it?" she asked. "You're thinking about something and it's not a good something."

"Yeah. I've just got a bad feeling about everything."

She turned and frowned. "What do you mean?"

"I wasn't going to say anything, but in light of our current situation, I don't think I should keep this to myself."

Kate stilled and narrowed her eyes at him. "What is it?"

"Someone slashed my tires. I need to go

take a look at your vehicle. I didn't have time to do that yet."

She gaped then snapped her mouth shut. "Slashed your tires? Great. That must have been what Cocoa and I interrupted on our early-morning outing."

"That's what I think. I'm going to see if he made it to your car or if you chased him off before he could get to it."

She nodded. "I'll come with you."

Kate appreciated the fact that he didn't bother to protest. She grabbed her coat, hat and gloves and followed him, still holding the bag. Angel and Cocoa bolted after them, biting at the flakes that fell from the gray sky.

She trailed him to the lean-to, where the deputy had parked her car. Lucas knelt and brushed the snow from the tires. "Well, they're fine." He stood and frowned, hands planted on his hips. His nose twitched, and his gaze shifted to the ground. "Do you smell fish?"

She'd noticed it but hadn't thought much about it. "Yes. Why?"

He dropped once more to the ground next to the car and pointed. Snow had blown into the lean-to and under the car, but she could see what had captured his attention. A yellow stain tainted the pristine white. "What's that?"

"Brake fluid. It has a fishy smell."

"Someone cut the brake line," she said. "It's sad that I'm not even shocked. But why go to all the trouble to strand us up here? I don't understand. All you have to do is call for help, right?"

Angel bounded over, her nose twitching. She sniffed around the tire then walked over to Kate and nudged the bag with the bunny. "What's she doing?"

"I'm not sure, but I think she's gotten the scent."

"From the car?"

"Yeah. Whoever cut the brake line had to touch the car, and I think Angel's picked up on it. Smells the same as the bunny, maybe."

"Has she ever done anything like that before?"

"No, but I'm going to let her go with it."

Hope surged. "Then we have another chance to find him? Or Chloe?"

"Maybe." He took the bag from her and gave Angel another whiff. "Let's see what you've got, girl."

After his sister had died, Lucas had always been skeptical of second chances but looked for them and accepted them whenever he had a chance to do so. He looked at Kate. "Go put Cocoa in the cabin. She won't be able to keep up with us."

"Okay." She spun and raced to the cabin with Cocoa in her arms.

When she returned less than a minute later, Lucas let Angel get another sniff of the bunny then said, "Angel, seek."

The dog took off and Lucas grabbed Kate's hand. "Stay close."

Kate clutched his fingers, and they followed after the border collie. Angel's nose often lifted then lowered, catching the scent from the air and the ground. Her tail wagged with the enthusiasm of the chase, and she took them into the trees.

And up.

"Where's she going?" Kate asked.

"I don't know. He came this way at some point." Before or after he'd attacked Kate? The climb up the side of the mountain required more effort than he would have thought. "How's your head?"

"Pounding, but I'll survive."

He had no doubt. She'd proven over and over that she was a survivor, and he had nothing but respect for that. Still, he hated that she felt she had to join in the chase. Then again, if he'd been in her shoes, he'd be doing the exact same thing. He was also okay with the fact that if she was with him, he could keep her as safe as possible.

Just ahead to his left, a noise captured his attention. A low snort, a huff of breath. Then the smell hit him.

Angel paused, spun toward the sound, and her hackles rose. She dropped her head and growled.

Kate stilled. "What is it?" she whispered.

A flash of black between the thick trees froze him. "Pretty sure that's a bear." The words left his lips and the animal rose on its hind legs, clicked its teeth and huffed then dropped back to all fours. It shook its head and ambled toward them.

"Angel, heel." Angel backed toward him, her eyes never leaving the approaching bear. "Back up, Kate. Slow and easy." She was a wildlife artist. She'd know what to do.

"Don't make eye contact with it," she whispered. "They see that as a sign of aggression."

"Yeah." He moved his hand into his pocket and removed his bear spray. "Come on, big guy. Just go on about your business. Please."

The bear spotted him, and Lucas kept the animal in his sights out of the corner of his eye.

"Lucas," she said, her voice so low he almost didn't hear it.

"Here, take Angel's leash and just keep walking."

She took it from him. "Angel, come."

The bear stopped, sniffed the air then studied them once more. "It's a black bear," Kate said. "You probably know that they don't usually charge. Lots of bluffing, but no charging. As long as we keep moving away from it, we should be okay."

"That's the hope."

He backed up as well, keeping the spray aimed in the bear's direction. The animal clicked its tongue and snorted but finally turned around and strolled away.

Lucas let out a slow breath of relief and spun to find Kate and Angel a good distance away, but obviously waiting on him. She wasn't going to leave him to face the bear alone. She'd probably only gone as far as she had to keep Angel from attracting the bear's attention.

He joined her and held the bunny out to Angel. "I don't know if she'll pick up the scent again, but we'll try."

Fifteen minutes later, Lucas finally conceded that Angel wasn't going to get the scent. He sighed and shook his head while Kate blinked rapidly, like she was fighting tears. Then she hardened her jaw. "At least it's stopped snowing for the moment," she said.

"For the moment. We'll count our blessings where we can get them."

"I'm hungry. You?"

"Starved." But he was also worried. "I need to call Tyson and give him an update. I know you're not a fan of leaving now that we've just figured out Chloe may be in the area, but Tyson may want to move you simply to make sure we can keep you safe. And that means we're going to have to figure out how to get off this mountain." He was going to have to work on that regardless.

"We're sitting ducks, aren't we?" she asked.

"Well… I wasn't going to put it quite that way, but yeah." Together, they walked back the way they came, fighting the snow and the frustration at another dead end. "The good thing is," he said, "the dogs will alert us to anyone who gets too close to the cabin. I've got the satellite phone, so we should have help soon."

She stopped and pointed. "Hey, Lucas. Check that out through those trees. Is that another cabin?"

"Well, what do you know? Looks like we have neighbors after all." He walked toward it with Kate trailing behind him.

She waded through the snow to the nearest window and cleaned it with her glove. "I think it's empty."

He mimicked her actions and peered through another window to get a different angle. The furnishings, while covered in plastic, looked ready to greet whoever walked through the door. "It's possible it's a seasonal home." He pointed to the sign on the door. "'I'd rather be golfing in Florida.' I don't think it's a stretch to assume that's where they are this time of year."

"I wouldn't mind that myself," she muttered.

He nodded his agreement then walked around the corner of the home to spot a shed next to a two-car detached garage. Not exactly sure what he was hoping to find—a farm truck or even a tractor would be an improvement over their current transportation troubles—he hurried to the large door and found it padlocked. He walked to the window, wiped the snow off, and peered in and spotted two snowmobiles. "Oh yes. Yes, yes. Thank You, Lord." He meant that prayer with every fiber of his being.

He dug in the snow for a minute until he found a rock that he thought might work. "Sorry about this," he muttered to the absent homeowners. He turned back to the lock and slammed the rock on it. It took two more tries before the padlock slipped off and fell to the ground.

Kate stepped up beside him. "What are you doing?"

"Something I'm going to have to make right later."

"What do you mean?"

"Snowmobiles. With ski gear hanging on the wall across from them. We won't need the bibs and boots and other stuff, but the masks and goggles will come in handy."

Her eyes went wide. "Okay. We're stealing them?"

"*Borrowing* them. I fully intend to return them—both with full tanks of gas—along with a new lock for the door." He sighed. "It's a way off the mountain, Kate—one other than walking in the freezing cold openly exposed to anyone who might like to use us for target practice."

"I'm fine with borrowing them."

He touched her cheek in thanks then asked, "Can you drive one?"

"Of course. We used to vacation in Aspen. My parents enjoy all kinds of winter sports, believe it or not. My nanny taught me to ski, snowboard and drive one of those." Sadness flickered in her gaze, then she shot him a forced smile. "I did have some amazing childhood experiences in spite of my loneliness and lack of parental presence." She gave a firm nod. "Hopefully it's like riding a bike and I'll remember everything."

He squeezed her hand. "It'll come back to you." He tried the light switch and grimaced when nothing happened. He tapped the flashlight app on his phone and sent the beam around the area. He spotted keys on a hook by the door. "Let's see if these work." He took a set over to the nearest machine, inserted the key and twisted.

Nothing. "Great," he muttered. He tried the other machine. Still nothing. "Ugh," he said, his heart sinking.

"Well, it was a good try," Kate said.

"I'm not giving up yet. It may need gas." Or a battery. Please, not a battery. "Most people keep extra gas—especially in this area. Can you use the light on your phone and look around and see if you can find a can of some?"

"Of course." While she looked, Lucas twisted the gas cap. Hard. It moved slowly then spun off into his hand. "Aha!"

"What did you find?" She called from a corner of the shed.

"Gunk on the gas cap—and definitely low on fuel. Once I clean this off and fill the tanks, we should be good." He hoped. "Now I just need something to clean it with."

"There's a whole stockpile of cleaning stuff over here on the shelves along the back wall as well as two full cans of gas like you figured." She shivered and scratched Angel's ears. "They stored everything really well." She waved a rag at him, and he walked over to see what she'd found. "You think that will get the snowmobiles working?" she asked.

"Yeah, I do. Wouldn't hurt to say a prayer, though."

"I've been doing that nonstop for a while now."

He glanced at her, wishing he could reassure her that everything was going to be okay. Instead of offering words he couldn't be sure were the truth, all he could do was his best to simply make it happen. He walked to the shelves and stared at the supplies. "Okay, I can use these…" He grabbed a roll of paper towels and set them aside, then scanned the labels on the cans. "Here we go. Denatured alcohol. Should do the trick."

He opened it and some sloshed out and down the side of the can, but most made it onto the piece of paper towel. He started to put the can back down when it slipped from his grasp and hit the ground with a loud clatter.

Kate sucked in a harsh breath as the fumes rose around them. He turned. "I'm sor—" The look on her face stopped him. "Kate? What is it? Talk to me."

But his words floated away, bouncing off whatever torment Kate had found herself lost in.

TEN

That smell…she knew it. It took her to a place in her mind that had been inaccessible up to this point, but the images clicked one after the other.

She drove her blue Honda Accord around a sharp curve of a mountain road. The darkness pressed in, heavy, ominous, making it hard to drag in breaths. Mentally, she knew it was simply the anxiety and fear crushing her lungs, but still she fought to pull in air. She had to get away, get somewhere safe.

A baby's piercing cry broke through the chaos of her thoughts. Chloe! In the back seat. Strapped into her carrier, clutching her little pink bunny. So much pink.

Then she was stopped. Why had she stopped?

Almost before the question formed, she had a vision of taillights behind her, getting closer and closer, shoving her toward the edge of the road. She'd slammed on the brakes, scared to get in a car wreck with the baby in the back.

A man approached the car, and the hackles on her neck rose with each step he took, drawing closer. He had something in his hand. Fear exploded through her, and she shoved out of the car, her only thought to protect the baby.

"What do you want?" She'd screamed the words at him. "Stop! I have a baby here."

He didn't answer, just swung the can at her. She ducked, launched herself at him, punching, scratching, screaming...

Chloe's cries echoed in the darkness.

Her attacker had tossed her aside without a word. Her head slammed into something, stunning her. Blackness swirled, but... Chloe! Nausea churned, and she watched the man splash something from the can all over the car. The pungent chemical smell assaulted her, the pain in her head blinded her and the darkness crept closer. Chloe's cries were the last thing she remembered before she blacked out.

"Kate! Kate, talk to me. Are you all right?" Lucas's hand gripped her bicep. He gave her a firm shake, pulling her from the memories.

Memories!

She gasped, stifling a sob. Relief rose within her at finally remembering. "I saw it," she said. "I remember more."

"What? Tell me."

She did. Every last detail. "He took her," she said in conclusion, "and now we've got to find *him*."

"Who?"

She shook her head, and tears threatened to choke her. She swallowed them, drawing strength from her rising anger. "I don't know who he was. I'd never seen him before, I don't think. He was wearing a mask and never spoke a word. He just doused the car with that stuff." She gestured to the denatured alcohol can. "I was very close to passing out when I saw him do that. He probably thought he'd killed me." He'd definitely come very close to succeeding. She touched the healed area on her head, the place she'd cracked against the rough asphalt. "She's here somewhere close by. I feel sure of it. I think subconsciously I knew that and that's why I wanted to come here so bad."

"Then there's something else you're not fully remembering."

"Yes." She frowned. "I agree, but I think it's close to the surface. I really think I'm on the tip of remembering why I needed to be here. In this area."

He nodded. "All right. That's good. Let's get these snowmobiles back to the house. I'll update Tyson on everything and let him know we're going to need some backup headed this way ASAP."

"I'd like to call Bryan and Skylar when you're finished if that's okay."

"Of course."

"They'll be super excited for me. Bryan may even have some more tips on how to pull the other memories to the surface."

"Perfect." He looked at Kate. "Can you hold the door and I'll maneuver these out of the shed?"

She shoved the door open and waited while he drove the first machine out into the open then went back for the second. Then she shut the doors and placed the broken lock through the loop. It wouldn't keep anyone out, but it would help keep the door from blowing open in the wind. She turned back to the snowmobile and found Lucas waiting for her. She climbed on hers and Lucas clicked to Angel, who bounded to his side.

He set her in front of him on the seat and wrapped the leash around his waist. With arms on either side of her, he trapped her against his chest, allowing him to see around her and control the machine at the same time. "Hang on, girl." To Kate, he asked, "Are you ready?"

She pulled the goggles down. "Lead the way. I'm right behind you."

When they pulled to a stop at the front of the cabin, she pointed to the porch light. "Hey, look. The power's back on."

"Well, things are looking up. Between finding the snowmobiles and the power, it's been a good day."

"In spite of the bad stuff?"

He shrugged. "We're still alive and your memory is coming back. It's good."

"True. I need to focus on the good stuff, don't I?"

"It helps when it seems like only bad stuff is happening." Lucas looked at the snowmobiles with a frown.

"What are you thinking about?" she asked.

"How to secure them. I've learned my lesson with the cars. I don't want someone sneaking in here and doing something to these."

"Maybe, at this point, it would be best to go stay in town near the sheriff's office?"

He nodded. "That's something we might want to think about now that we're mobile."

Once back inside the cabin, Cocoa greeted Kate like she'd been gone for days instead of hours. Lucas released Angel from her work gear, and she went to her water bowl for a long drink.

Kate gave Cocoa a short belly rub then shrugged out of her coat and gloves and walked into her side of the duplex to throw another log on the fire. Who knew how long the power would last. She had a feeling it would go off again at some point. "I'm going to call Skylar and Bryan while I can. Then I'll throw together something to eat, okay?"

"Sounds good. I'm going to try Tyson on the sat phone."

Kate headed for the cordless handset on the end table and dialed. The Denver PD detective always answered on the first or second ring, and Kate appreciated that she never had to wonder if the woman was going to answer or not. If she didn't know any better, she'd suspect that Skylar was sitting around just waiting for the phone to ring. It didn't take her long to fill Skylar in. "I really think I'm going to remember soon."

"I sure hope so, my friend. I can only imagine how hard this has been on you."

"Thank you."

"Have you talked to your therapist?"

"He's next on the list." She walked into
the kitchen and pulled items from the refrigerator to prepare a chef's salad. Thankfully,
the small generator kept the refrigerator running in spite of the power outage. "But I just
wanted to say thank you for everything. I
know the only reason I'm still alive is because
of you and the team. Lucas has been an answer to a prayer. I honestly don't know what
I'd do without him."

"Hang in there, Kate. I really think this is
going to be over soon."

"I sure hope so."

They hung up, and Kate walked to the
window to look out. All she could see was
white. The snow was probably around eigh-
teen inches deep at this point. Normally, she'd
enjoy the powdery fun, but now that she knew
that the person who wanted her dead was
aware of her location, the snow just made
her feel trapped.

She spun away from the window and
grabbed the phone to dial Bryan's number.
That the therapist was just a phone call away

helped ward off the panic attack. Although, she had to admit being in Lucas's company, and feeling more safe than she had in months, had gone a long way toward getting rid of the attacks and nightmares.

"Hello?"

"Bryan? This is Kate. Again."

"Kate, good to hear from you. How are you doing?"

"I'm all right."

"I've missed our in-person chats. Are you planning on returning any time soon?"

She sighed. "As soon as we find the person who'd like to kill me."

"I just can't believe this is happening to you. I'm so sorry. Is there anything I can do?"

At his soft, kind words, more anxiety seeped from her. She did have people who cared about her. Somehow, she was going to live through this. "No, Bryan, nothing. Thank you." She paused. "In fact, I think I'm going to be all right."

"Of course you are."

"No, I mean, I don't think I need you anymore." Silence greeted her, and she hurried to soften her words. "I'm sorry. I didn't mean that in a bad way. In fact, it's meant in a very *good* way. You did what you set out to do. Help me deal with getting my memories back."

"You remember *everything*?"

"No, not exactly." Like the reason she wanted to come to Montana. Why couldn't she remember that? Was she just making that up? She sighed. At this point, she was going to assume that it wasn't that important. "Anyway, I'm so thankful, but the truth is, while I remember what happened that night, I still don't know who caused the wreck, set my car on fire and stole Chloe. He's just a masked figure in my memories."

"So, you never actually saw him?"

"Well, I saw him. I just never saw his face. So, there's really nothing left to remember about that. Even if I hadn't hit my head and had a concussion, I never would have been able to identify the person who did all that. But my gut tells me that it's the same person who attacked me in the rental house. I couldn't testify to that in court, of course, not based on a feeling, but…"

Lucas peered into the room and she waved at him, noting he was wearing his weapon on his hip. His brows were drawn into a frown, and his shoulders were set with tension. He was worried about her. She motioned that she was almost done, and he nodded, glanced at her door—no doubt-checking to make sure she'd turned the dead bolt—threw another log on the fire for her, then disappeared back in to his side.

"I'm not sure we should go our separate ways just yet, Kate," Bryan said, a thread of tension in his words that she didn't really understand. Was he worried about losing the income? It wasn't like he had a shortage of clients. "I'd really like to keep talking with you," he said, "even if it's just over the phone, so that I'm here if you need me."

She thought about that for a brief moment. What was the harm in it? If she needed him, he'd be there. If she didn't…well, then that was fine, too. The truth was she'd much rather talk with Lucas than Bryan. But… Lucas wasn't a trained counselor and Bryan was. And Bryan had helped her up to this point. "All right. I'm okay with that. I'll be in touch."

"Great. I'm glad you agree, Kate. Are you sure you don't want to come into the office?"

She pictured the weather outside the little cabin and smiled. "That's not possible at the moment, but I'll let you know."

"Where are you anyway?"

"Safe." For the moment. "Goodbye, Bryan. Talk to you later."

"All right. Bye, Kate."

She hung up and finished putting the meal together—grateful for the gas stove in case the power went out in the middle of cooking—with the occasional glance out the window. For now, things were quiet, but the hair standing on the back of her neck said she was simply in the eye of the storm. Someone wanted her dead, and he wasn't giving up on making that happen any time soon.

Lucas had called Tyson and had to wait for him to get back in touch with him. In the meantime, he gave Kate her privacy and paced the floor, keeping an eye on the snowmobiles. He'd checked in with Skylar after she got off the phone with Kate.

"What do you think, Skylar? I know you and the team are still investigating full speed ahead. Why can't we find any leads on this?"

"I honestly don't know. I'm leaning more and more toward this having to do with Nikki and her background."

"You mean Chloe's father?"

"It's the only thing that makes sense. We've exhausted every other avenue, every lead, every single possibility. We've talked to every friend we could track down, and no one could give us a clue, much less a name, but it's the one piece of information missing."

"Who Chloe's father is."

"Yes. Whatever Nikki was involved in has bled over onto Kate. And without that missing piece…"

"Yeah." He rubbed a hand over the back of his neck, thinking. "All right, I'll go back to Kate and see if she can find a way to pull that memory from her brain. But if Nikki never said, then…"

"Right. I know. If the memory isn't there to start with, then there's no point in trying to find one."

His phone buzzed with an incoming call. "Hey, I've got to go. Tyson is calling."

"Sure. Bye, Lucas."

He hung up and switched lines. "Tyson, thanks for getting back to me." He reported their current situation.

"All right," Tyson said, "I will try and get someone out to the cabin for added security, but with the weather predicted to only get worse over the next couple of hours, I can't guarantee it."

"I know, but the sheriff might be able to help. He's got it together."

"I'll touch base with him."

"Thanks."

"But, Lucas, don't count on help, okay?"

"I know. I've already thought about that."

"Hang tight. I'll be back in touch soon. I've got an idea, but again, can't guarantee it will go anywhere."

They ended the call and Lucas sighed. He was going with the assumption that he and Kate were pretty much on their own. Not exactly the best news, but Lucas would work with it. If help couldn't get through, neither could anyone else. Right?

Maybe.

It depended on where they were located. The temps were dropping with the sun.

He peered into her little den area and found her wrapped in a blanket, sitting by the fire. She had her sketchbook in her lap, and her hand moved across the page, the pencil making scratching noises that he found oddly comforting. Angel snoozed at her feet and Cocoa had snuggled up under Angel's belly, taking advantage of the body heat. The whole scene was way too cozy. If he wasn't careful, he was going to find it hard to say goodbye to Kate. Just the thought made him frown.

Ever since his team had been called in to assist with her case, Kate had been in his life. For eight months, there hadn't been a day that had gone by without him thinking about her in one way or another. His emotions had run the gamut on her behalf. From furious that someone had tried to kill her to worried that she wouldn't wake up. And now that she had, he was terrified he wouldn't be able to keep her safe and find Chloe. Which meant he needed to keep a clear head and make the right decisions. For her. If that meant keeping his distance in order to keep his perspective, then that's what he would have to do.

He cleared his throat, and she looked up. A lock of hair fell across her cheek, and the soft smile that curved her lips sent his heart spinning. So much for distance and perspective.

"Hey," she said. "Everything all right?"

"At the moment. What are you drawing?"

Her smile turned sad, and he almost wished he hadn't asked. "Chloe. I think about her all the time. Wondering what she's like now. If she still hates her feet covered or if she would remember the song I used to sing to her. This is how I remember her at three months old."

She turned the tablet around so he could see it, and he blinked at the lifelikeness of the image.

"Kate, that's incredible. You did all of that with just a pencil?"

She ducked her head, but he could tell his praise touched her. Pleased her. Maybe embarrassed her a little. "I did. Once you learn the techniques, it's not terribly hard."

"Not terribly hard for someone with a gift like yours maybe, but for someone like me who has trouble drawing a stick figure, well…"

She laughed, and he had to turn away from the brilliance of her smile. He liked the look in her eyes then, at the moment lacking the fear and tension that always seemed to be there.

"I stayed with Nikki for several weeks after Chloe was born," she said, her voice quiet in the room. Angel's soft snores and the fire crackling in the fireplace were the only other sounds he could discern. The cabin was so well-built that even the wind outside was barely there.

"I'm sure she appreciated that."

"She did. She was a good mother. Patient and good to Chloe. She loved her fiercely. Of course, she was also tired and still recovering from giving birth, but she was determined to give Chloe a great life." She chuckled. "One thing that neither of us could get over was the fact that when Chloe was at her fussiest, I was always the one who could get her to go to sleep. I'd hold her and sing to her and she'd just watch me like I was the greatest thing in the world."

"I can understand that," he murmured before he could stop the words from leaving his lips. But Kate had a faraway look in her eyes, and he wasn't sure she even heard him. Then the faraway look morphed into a sadness so poignant that his own throat tightened.

"Hey, you feel like a game of Scrabble?" he asked.

She blinked and focused in on him. "Are you trying to distract me?"

"Maybe just a little."

She set aside her drawing and nodded, the shadows in her eyes lightening a fraction. "Sure, that would be fun. I don't think I'll have any trouble staying awake for it."

"Yeah, me either, but we're going to have to try to get some rest at some point."

She bit her lip and her eyes clouded again. "What if he shows up while we're sleeping?"

"Angel will let us know if anyone gets close. And if Angel starts barking, Cocoa will probably join in, too."

"True."

He snagged the game from the shelf on the television stand and set it on the kitchen table. "Come on."

"I'm not sure you want to do this." She shot him a small smirk.

He grinned. "Why? You think you can beat me?"

"Well…"

"Oh, I see how it is. You're on." Lucas was glad to see the fear fade once more. She didn't have to know he was on edge and listening for even a hint that someone might be outside. As he'd said, he felt sure the dogs would alert them if that was the case, but it didn't mean he was dropping his guard.

ELEVEN

Three hours later, Kate yawned. She'd beat him in two out of three games, but he was definitely a worthy opponent. "You've played a lot, haven't you?" she asked.

He smiled. "My dad and I used to play quite a bit. How'd you get so good?"

"I hated English and my tutor used Scrabble as a way to help me with my vocabulary. She said if I could find a way to work in all of my spelling words—and got them right—I didn't have to take her test. She was sneaky like that."

"Sounds like you had some really great people in your life in spite of your parents' absence."

"I did. I'm very fortunate, I know." She packed up the game and slid it back on the shelf. Angel raised her head and Cocoa snuggled closer to her friend. Kate scratched both dogs' ears then turned to Lucas. "I hate that you feel like you had to stay awake and keep me company."

Lucas raised a brow at her. "Are you kidding? This is the most fun I've had in a long time."

"Scrabble? With me?" She dropped into the chair beside him and gave him a light punch on his bicep. "You seriously need to reevaluate your social life."

He grasped her hand and she stilled. Then swallowed hard while her stomach flipped and her pulse tripped into high gear. He continued to hold her hand—and her eyes. Then his gaze dipped to her lips for a fraction of a second before he set her hand free and cleared his throat. "I guess I've been such a workaholic that I haven't really taken much time to socialize lately. The training sessions were good and there were a lot of really great people involved…"

"But?" Had he thought about *kissing* her? Because the thought of him leaning over and doing so didn't bother her *at all*. In fact, she had a suspicion that it would be a thrilling experience.

But he'd backed off, and now he shrugged. "They were strangers, people I'll probably never see again. Or at least not any time soon. It's easy to be friendly and outgoing for a few days with people I don't know. And I guess it *is* fun in a work kind of way."

"What about the others in the K-9 Unit? You're close to them, aren't you?"

"Yeah, I'd call them friends, but…" He shrugged. "I don't know. We keep stuff mostly work related."

"They do or you do?"

He tilted his head. "Hmm. It's kind of scary that you can read me as well as you do, but… you're right. I probably do more than they do."

"Hmm." She mimicked him with a teasing glance. "Imagine that."

He shot her a slow smile. "You're a special person, you know that, Kate?"

She blinked. "I am?"

His smile faded. "Yes, and I think it's sad that you don't recognize it."

"Well, I mean, I don't have a terrible self-esteem or anything thanks to my art teacher and a few other lovely people, but I guess I've never really thought of myself as…special."

He squeezed her hand. "You've been through so much in the last several months, and you're still standing. Still fighting back.

You're brave, courageous even, and yet you haven't developed a cynical hardness that I think a lot of people would—as a defense mechanism. Which would be totally understandable, and…well…" He shrugged. "I could go on, but trust me, Kate, you're special. I've never known anyone like you."

He'd rendered her speechless. As heat crept into her cheeks, something she'd never felt before slipped into her heart. Something that might just be more than like and admiration for the man in front of her. "You're pretty special yourself, Lucas."

Several seconds passed, and he seemed to fight a battle with himself before he leaned forward and grazed her lips with his. Kate lifted a hand to cup the back of his head and kept her eyes locked on his. He hesitated, then reached up and removed her hand from his neck. "I'm…well, I'm not sorry exactly, but I probably shouldn't have done that."

"Why not?" Kate refused to feel rejected. He was attracted to her or he wouldn't have kissed her. There was something else going on with him.

"Because if I allow myself to be distracted—as lovely a distraction that it would be—I might not be as alert as I should be."

"Alert to danger," she said softly.

"Yes."

Kate sat back. "Has that happened before?"

He turned and pursed his lips. "No. Not like this. Nothing like this."

"Tell me, Lucas. I can see in your eyes that you want to get close to me, but something holds you back. Something more than just the job."

He sighed and turned to lean against the wall. "I guess I owe you an explanation."

"Not at all. You don't *owe* me anything."

"Maybe 'owe' is the wrong word. Shana, my ex-wife, was someone Angel and I helped find and rescue off the side of a mountain. She and some friends had lost their way and gotten trapped." He shrugged. "I was her hero and she let me know it. My head got a little too big, and I tumbled into a whirlwind relationship with her. We got married, and it turned out that the reality of my job wasn't nearly as romantic as she'd built it up to be in her head. She refused counseling and found someone else."

"I'm so sorry, Lucas."

"Yeah. I am, too." He raked a hand over his head. "I'm past her. I don't love her anymore. Honestly, I'm not sure I ever did. I loved the idea of her. We married for all the wrong reasons, and it didn't work out."

"And you've never been tempted to try again?"

"No way. No one's been worth the risk of that kind of hurt again." He cleared his throat. "So, now you know the whole ugly story. And why I can't—we can't—well, I just can't let myself get distracted. By you. By anything."

"I understand." And she did. It didn't mean it didn't hurt, but he was right. Distractions for either of them right now wouldn't be a good idea. And besides, she wasn't certain she was in any frame of mind to be getting romantically involved with anyone. She came with a lot of baggage. Was it fair to ask Lucas to deal with it?

A shaft of pain pierced her. Cocoa sat up and yawned then trotted over to jump up in her lap. Kate snuggled the little mutt close, and Lucas rose to look out the window. "I guess it's probably time we tried to get some sleep."

"Sure."

He turned. "Kate, I didn't mean to hurt your feelings—or lead you on, or anything else you may be thinking. I just—"

"You don't have anything to apologize for."

He didn't look like he believed her. "I promise, Lucas. We're fine. You're a good man in a difficult position. I appreciate you being honest and putting my safety first. That says a lot about your character."

He tilted his head and a small smile curved his lips. "Like I said before, you're a pretty special person." Before she could respond, he walked over to the connecting door and looked back. She followed his gaze. Angel hadn't moved from her spot in front of the fire. "I guess she's sleeping here tonight if you're okay with that," he said.

"Of course. Just leave the door cracked in case she wants to come to your side."

"I can do that. Take care of her for me."

Kate froze, the words echoing in her mind. *Take care of her, Kate. Promise you'll take care of her.* She gasped.

"Kate?" Lucas asked. "What is it? What's wrong?"

"I remember something else."

"What?" He strode over and knelt in front of her. "Tell me."

"That phrase…'take care of her for me'… Nikki said that very thing then put Chloe in my arms."

Lie low. Be safe. Whatever you do, don't

let them get her. They can't have her, you un-derstand?

"Who can't have her?" Lucas asked, and Kate realized she'd said the words out loud.

Tears gathered behind her lids, and she forced them back. Crying would solve noth-ing and just make her head hurt. She sniffed. "I don't know. I don't remember if she ever told me." She swiped a hand over her eyes then met his gaze. "But she was terrified of whoever it was."

"Then if you can remember who she was so scared of, it's possible we'll know who has Chloe."

"I know, I know." She pressed her fingers to her lids. "But I don't think she told me. I seriously think I've remembered every-thing, and she never told me who I was to keep Chloe safe *from.*"

He frowned. "Then how would you know who to keep her away from?"

She sighed and shook her head. "I think she might have been about to tell me, but… we heard an engine."

"When you were meeting in the park?"

"Yes. And it spooked her so bad she gave me Chloe then ran. When she ran, I did, too. With Chloe strapped in the back seat."

"And the person caught up with you and…"

"And tried to kill me." She pressed her palms to her eyes. "Later, when I woke from the coma, it was to learn Nikki was dead."

"I know. They found her shortly after you were taken to the hospital." He rubbed her shoulder. "I'm so sorry."

"I feel like I should be able to figure this out."

"Maybe some sleep will help?"

"Maybe."

She rose and Lucas did, too. "Good night, Kate. I'll be watching, and so will Angel. We're going to figure this out soon. I can feel it."

Kate nodded but couldn't help wondering if it would be before or after the person trying to kill her managed to do so.

Lucas threw more wood on the fire burning on his side of the cabin, clutched his weapon and scanned the darkness. Angel had finally joined him and rested in her bed next to the fireplace. She wasn't worried, which meant he could probably relax and grab a couple of hours of sleep before the sun decided to rise.

The silence from the other side of the duplex suggested Kate had found a way to fall asleep, so Lucas settled on the couch, got comfortable and closed his eyes. At least the couch was between his door and Kate's, so in the unlikely event that someone managed to get inside, it wouldn't take him long to get to her.

When he returned to awareness, it was to the smell of coffee and the sound of sizzling bacon. He pushed off the blanket he'd snagged during the three hours he'd slept and rose. After a quick brush of his teeth and hair, he grabbed Angel's leash and walked to the connecting door to knock.

"Come in," Kate called.

He pushed through and found her standing in front of the fire with a mug in her hand. Dark shadows rimmed her eyes, but she shot him a small smile. "Good morning."

"Morning."

"Did you get some sleep?"

"A few hours. You?"

"The same."

The small talk helped settle him, and he nodded to her coffeepot. "You mind? It would be nice not to have to wait the sixty seconds it would take to brew some."

Another smile flickered at him before it disappeared. "Of course not."

Once he had his own mug in hand, he went to the window and looked out. Barely stifling his groan at the landscape of white, he turned to find Kate in her same spot. "You okay?"

She nodded. "I guess. I dreamed about Nikki last night and have been thinking about her ever since I opened my eyes."

"And?"

"She was so excited when she found out she was having a girl. She would have been fine with a boy, but even in college, she talked about how fun it would be to have a daughter. Nikki decided right then that everything would be pink. Pink crib, pink bedding, pink mobile, pink clothing, pink diapers when she could find them. She even had pink carpet put in Chloe's room."

Lucas hoped he hid his grimace. "That's a lot of pink."

"It was entirely *too much* pink." Kate laughed. "But Nikki was Nikki, and once she made up her mind that pink would be Chloe's color, she went all out." Kate shook her head. "But that's not what I've been thinking about the most. I've been going over every single conversation we had since resuming our friendship."

He peered out the window once more then

leaned a shoulder against the wooden wall. "And have you come up with anything that might help us find Chloe?"

"No. At least nothing I can put my finger on."

"Why don't you tell me what you've been thinking? Sometimes talking it out can trigger other memories."

"Once again, you sound like my therapist." She sighed. "But I'm game. Nikki didn't have a great relationship with her mother, but when Mrs. Baker was diagnosed with cancer shortly before Nikki became pregnant with Chloe, Nikki dropped everything to help her. She took her to her treatments, helped arrange for a wig when she lost her hair to the chemo—and more."

"Sounds like she was a good person."

"She was in the end." A small, sad smile curved her lips. "But when we were in college, Nikki was quite the wild one. Nothing too over the top, but she had her moments. Nikki was very pretty and had this bubbly, outgoing personality that everyone loved— especially the guys. No was immune it seemed like."

"Tell me more about her, growing up with her. How did you two meet? I keep thinking that it's an unlikely friendship due to your parents' feelings about propriety and who you should be friends with." Lucas decided pushing for a little more information couldn't hurt. The more he knew about Nikki, the better.

"Oh my. So many stories. Well, my parents didn't like her very much, that was for sure, especially after some of her antics landed her in hot water with authorities."

"What do you mean?" Authorities? "Tell me about that."

Kate hesitated. "Let me start at the beginning. So, Nikki's family and mine went to the same church. Nikki and I were in fifth-grade Sunday school one morning when AJ South shoved me down on the playground. Nikki gave him a bloody nose, and we were best friends from then on. At least we tried to be."

"Sounds like a loyal friend."

"Yeah," Kate whispered. "I miss her."

"What did she do to get arrested?" Could the current situation be so simple as to having something to do with Nikki's past troubles when she and Kate were kids?

"Oh, that." She cleared her throat. "Once, when we were about fifteen, Nikki decided she wanted to prove her artistic skills were better than mine—and that she was more creative."

He raised a brow. "I can't imagine that."

"She decided she would show the world, so she bought some spray paint and headed down to a bridge. She spray-painted graffiti all over it. Funny stuff about her teachers and friends. Nothing mean or obscene. She was actually a very clever artist." Admiration glinted in her gaze for a millisecond. "But she got caught. She picked a bridge that the local police patrolled on a regular basis, and they picked her up mid spray."

"What happened to her?"

"She got a lecture and a slap on the wrist. She had to do community service. She later laughed and told me she was officially a 'bad girl.'"

"Was she?"

"No, not really. She did go for the 'bad boys,' so to speak. The troubled, moody type. She'd tell me all their problems then ask me for advice on how to respond. Like *I* was a therapist."

"What kind of problems?"

Kate shrugged. "The usual teen stuff. Not getting along with their parents or siblings. Alcohol and drugs were sometimes an issue. That kind of stuff."

"What about more recently?"

"Now, that, I don't really know—" Kate paused with a frown "Wait a minute. There was one guy she dated…"

"Who?"

"I can't think of his name, but… Maddox?"

A tingle of excitement zipped through him. "Maddox. Okay. Is that a first name or a last name?" Because if it was a last name…

"Last, I think."

Lucas looked her in the eye. "Okay, this is really important, Kate."

"What?"

"Do you remember his first name?"

She rubbed a hand across her forehead. "I think it started with an S. Steven? Scott? Seth?" She sighed. "I don't know, but—" Her eyes went wide, and she dropped her hand. "Wait a minute. When the cops searched Nikki's apartment after her death, they found a gold watch with initials on the back. No one could figure out where such an expensive watch came from—whose it was or how Nikki got it. The initials were 'S.M.', weren't they?"

"Yeah."

"Sean!" The name burst from her. "Yes, Nikki mentioned him one time, and honestly, it seemed like an accident. Like his name slipped from her before she could stop it. That watch is his, isn't it? And he's probably Chloe's father. He has to be." Excitement glowed in her eyes. "I did it! I finally remembered!"

"Kate, are you sure? Like one-hundred percent sure?"

Some of her excitement dimmed. "As sure as I can be. Why?"

"Because the Maddox family is a big-time crime family."

TWELVE

Kate blinked. "Crime family? *Crime* family? That's who's behind all this?"

"I don't know that for a fact, but if Sean is Chloe's father, then yeah, probably."

"I… I don't know what to think. Or say."

"The Maddox family has been on the law enforcement radar for a long time. Four years ago, Lawson Maddox had a heart attack. Dropped dead at his trial."

She frowned. "I think I remember hearing about that."

"If it is Sean, then Nikki must have had a fling with him. He must have been pressuring her about seeing Chloe or trying to get custody or something." She stood to pace to the fireplace and back. "That's why she gave me Chloe and told me to keep her safe. It has to be." She looked at him. "Sean is behind this. If we find him, we find Chloe." Hope started to build once more. His deep sigh stopped her. "What?"

"I hate to tell you this, but it's not Sean after you. He's dead."

And just like that, the hope fizzled. She sank back onto the couch. "What?"

"He died in a car wreck late last year in Aspen." He paused. "Nikki would have been three months pregnant or so."

"Then who..." She closed her eyes, desperate to pull more details from her brain. "Nikki said, 'Take care of her for me.' And then added, 'Don't let them get to her.'" She opened her eyes. "Wait a minute. Them. She said *them*. Could she have meant the Maddox *family*?"

"I'd say that's a good possibility. If Sean knew he had a child and told his family, then... yeah. I don't think they'd just let her go."

Kate dropped her head into her hands, and Cocoa walked over to jump up next to her. Kate pulled the little dog next to her, taking comfort in her presence but also thinking. "So, what's the next step?"

"We alert the team that we think the Maddox family is involved in everything that's happened to you. They'll open an investigation and see if they can prove it one way or another. But if what you're saying is right, Kate, you're in over your head. We both are. And this safe house isn't going to be safe enough. You're going to need a lot more security than this."

Her stomach dropped. "We have to leave?"

"Yeah, I'd say so. The Maddox family has a lot of reach."

She nodded to the window. "But how do we get away? The snowmobiles?"

"Exactly. I'm going to load everything I can on there while you get ready. Do you have some kind of way to strap Cocoa to you?"

Kate thought of the pullover parka with the front-zip pocket. Cocoa would probably fit in there. "Yes. I think so."

"You get it and pack what you can carry. I'll call Tyson and let him know we're going to need a lot more protection on you than we originally thought."

"I'm sorry," she whispered. She hated feeling like a burden.

Lucas gripped her hand, set Cocoa on the floor and pulled her close for hug. She rested her cheek on his chest and listened to his strong heartbeat. "This isn't your fault, Kate," he said. "I know I keep saying that, but it's true, and I'll keep saying it until you believe it."

His words washed over her, and she bit her lip on the tears that rose to the surface. She was coming to care for this man way too much. And now she just learned that he was in even greater danger thanks to her. Danger so great that he wanted to call in a *team* to help protect her. "If this is all true," she said, "Nikki had to know what she'd be getting me in to by asking me to take Chloe. I can't believe she didn't say anything—or at least warn me."

"She probably planned to when she handed Chloe off to you. You said you were interrupted."

"Yes. We were. If our speculations are correct, then I guess we'll never know if she planned to tell me or not." She sighed and pulled back, wanting to stay right where she was but also knowing they needed to leave. "I'll get ready."

Lucas snagged the satellite phone. "I'll make the call to Tyson."

Kate hurried into the bedroom and threw her meager belongings into the backpack then pulled on the parka that would hold Cocoa. She heard Lucas's door open and close and figured he was packing the snowmobile. For the next several minutes, she packed only the necessary items that she could carry with her. She left the large easel, taking only her pencils and the sketchpad.

When she returned to the den, Angel was dressed back in her work gear, doggie snow boots and all, and snapped to the leash. Lucas's voice reached her from the other side of the duplex.

"Got it. We're going to head to the sheriff's office at the bottom of the mountain. We'll just sleep at the jail if we have to. Whatever it takes to ensure her safety."

Kate gaped. Sleep at the jail? This is what her life had become? She almost laughed. Almost. Wouldn't her parents have just loved *that*? Sadness chased away any levity she might have found in the situation, and she retreated to the kitchen to pack a container of dog food and thermos of water.

"You ready?" Lucas asked from the connecting door.

"Yes."

"All right, let's head for the—"

When he broke off, Kate raised a brow. "What?"

He held up a hand and walked to the window, standing to the side. She noticed this was a habit for him. "I hear an engine."

Dread sent her stomach aiming straight for her toes. No one in their right mind would be out in this kind of weather. "What kind of engine?"

He shook his head and pulled his weapon. "Stay here and—"

The window next to him exploded in a blast of gunfire.

Glass littered the floor—and the side of his face. Lucas ducked as pain shot through his cheek then lunged at Kate and pulled her to the floor, rolling her behind the couch. The dogs barked and raced to the door.

"Angel! Heel!"

"Cocoa! Come!"

His and Kate's voice blended. The dogs obeyed as another spate of gunfire erupted, taking out the lamp and decorating the sofa with an intermittent pattern of holes. Lucas tucked Angel to one side of him and hovered over Kate and Cocoa as much as he could. Growls rumbled in Angel's chest, and he could feel the tension running through her. Much like the same tension running through Kate.

"I guess they decided to come back," Kate said. Her words came across low and calm, but he heard the tinge of fury beneath them. The terror. The rage. Her breaths came in pants, and he figured she was holding on to her emotions by her fingernails.

"Yeah." The sound of the engine faded, and Lucas rolled to his feet. "That's it. I'm going after him."

"I'm right behind you."

He didn't bother to tell her to stay put. With Angel already in her working gear and all of their stuff on the snowmobiles, all they had to do was climb on and take off. He glanced out the window and saw nothing. Then opened the door. A figure twenty yards away stepped out from behind the trunk of a large tree and aimed a weapon in his direction. "Kate, get down!" He slammed the door, turned and dragged Kate to the floor once more. The bullet pierced the door, sending wood fragments flying.

The shooter's engine roared to life once more, and Lucas peered out the door to see the machine heading for the trees, the shooter hunched forward. "He's on the run!" Lucas bolted to his feet and out the door with Angel's leash clasped in his hand.

With fast, efficient movements, he got the dog settled in front him, her leash tied tight around him to ensure she didn't fall off in case of a tight turn, then looked at Kate. Cocoa was snuggled into the front pouch of the parka, her tiny black nose quivering in the opening. "Ready?"

She nodded, and he caught a glimpse of the shooter in the trees at the edge of the property. "There he is. Stay to the side of me, okay?"

"Yes."

Lucas gunned the motor and shot forward. He could hear Kate behind him and prayed she was as skilled on the snowmobile as she'd led him to believe. Whoever was driving the one fleeing was pretty good. The driver swerved in and out of the trees, keeping his balance and putting distance between him and Kate. "Hang on, Angel-girl. He's not getting away, and you're going to have your chance to go to work. We have a baby to find."

Angel barked then rested her snout on his shoulder.

He glanced back at Kate to see her bent forward, her scarf flapping in the wind. While he couldn't see her eyes behind the goggles, he could picture them, intent and determined. She, more than anyone, wanted to catch the person up ahead.

She gunned the engine, staying at Lucas's side. The machines were good, easy to steer and responsive to the lightest command. He knew she'd have no trouble keeping up, but unless the snowmobile they were chasing ran out of gas, he wasn't sure how they were going to be able to catch up.

She glanced at Lucas, and he nodded to the fork in the trees just ahead. "Go that way! Cut him off!"

She gunned the machine and whipped around the trees, gaining on the fleeing shooter.

Lucas could only pray that Kate understood what he was thinking. When she nodded and slanted her machine to the right, he breathed a little easier. "Yes," he whispered under his breath. She whipped past the trees while Lucas hummed in the other direction.

The shooter was ahead, aiming for the open field just beyond the tree line. As long as Kate could inch in front of him, he would have the guy hemmed in behind. The shooter would have no choice but to stop or head into the thick group of trees.

Kate gunned her snowmobile and swerved around a tree. Snow kicked up around her, but she had control of the big machine, and Lucas could almost picture the determination on her face. He drew closer to the person who'd tried to kill them, and the shooter looked back over his shoulder. Lucas wished he could see the face behind the mask and goggles, but the slender form under the bulky winter clothes made him do a double take. If he wasn't seeing things, he'd guess that the driver was a *woman*. He thought back to Kate describing a woman in the truck that had come after them days ago. This was clearly the thug's partner.

Maybe Sean Maddox's mother. Or sister. Someone in his family.

Kate closed in on the other side, and the woman whipped her head around. The shooter had nowhere to go. "Stop!" Lucas prayed she could hear him. The snowmobiles were loud, but the woman jerked at his shout, so he knew his voice reached her. She slowed slightly, and he thought she might stop completely, but then she gunned it and aimed for the trees then cut back like she was going to try and make a sharp turn through a narrow opening. Too narrow an opening. "No! Don't do it!"

Kate sped toward her, and the driver cut the machine too sharp, too close to the trees and slammed into the nearest one. The horrible screeching impact sent a wave of sickness through him. He pulled his own craft to a stop, aware that Kate had done the same. He untied Angel from him and looped her leash over the handlebar then ran toward the person on the ground, noticing the crushed helmet.

A groan reached him, and he slid to his knees beside her. "Hold still. I got you." He slipped the helmet from her head and winced at the battered face revealed. She had a head wound, but it wasn't that bad. What—?

"Lucas?" Kate's horrified whisper pulled his attention to the stain spreading in the pristine snow. It came from under the woman's back.

The shooter gasped, her eyes wide. She looked at Kate, and her gaze narrowed, the hate there piercing him before she sucked in another wheezing breath. A thin stream of blood dribbled from her mouth, and she went still, eyes fixed, pupils unresponsive.

Lucas checked her pulse and found nothing. "She's dead," he said. But what had killed her? The head wound looked bad, but where was the blood under her coming from?

He rolled her slightly and grimaced. She'd landed on a thick branch and impaled herself. She must have hit something vital because it hadn't taken her long to bleed out. He sighed and dropped his head, hating the way her life had ended.

"Who is she?" Kate asked. "Why would she want me dead? And is she the one who has Chloe?"

Kate's terrified questions spilled over him one after the other. "I don't know, Kate, but I think this is Tonya Maddox. Sean's mother." It was hard to tell with the head wound, but she looked familiar. Tyson had sent some information on the Maddox family as soon as they'd hung up. He pulled the sat phone from his pocket and found the message with the pictures.

"*That's* Tonya Maddox?" Kate asked. "You're sure?"

He held the screen up so she could see. "Pretty sure. The matriarch of the Maddox family. She and her two sons are the ones behind a lot of crime in this area. Well, one son now. His name is David. When Tonya's husband dropped dead, she picked up right where he left off." He studied the picture then the woman. "Even with her face bruised and battered, it still looks like her. Hold on a second." He patted her pockets and located a small wallet confirming his suspicions. "Yes, that's her."

He looked up to see tears fill Kate's eyes then spill over onto her cheeks.

"She took Chloe."

"Yes, I'm guessing she did."

"And now she's dead, and Chloe's still missing." She dropped to her knees and pressed her hands to her eyes. "We're never going to find her, are we?"

Lucas went to her and wrapped his arms around her. She buried her face in his shoulder. "Yes, we are. Somehow. Remember, she's working with someone. A man. Maybe her son, David. We'll find him. We'll find Chloe." He called Tyson, and the man answered on the second ring. He gave his sergeant the quick version of the most recent events. "Do you have someone who can come pick up the body?"

"It might take a while, but I'll get someone up there. Gonna need your statements, too."

"Of course." He looked around at the open clearing. "It's stopped snowing for the moment. I think a chopper could land here. It might be a little tight and depends on the wind, but I think it's possible." The pilot he'd flown with in Iraq could do it for sure.

He gave Tyson their location as close as he could figure. "She's got on a black snowsuit, so should be pretty easy to spot from the air."

"I'm on it."

They hung up, and Lucas spotted a hint of pink peeking out of one of Tonya's front pockets. He must have dislodged whatever it was when he'd rolled her. He snagged the cloth and pulled.

When he held it up, Kate's gasp drew his attention to her. "That's Chloe's. I mean, it's got to be."

"Why?"

"It's a bib. I think I've seen a picture of her wearing it."

He hesitated and looked at Angel still sitting patiently on the snowmobile. "Then this isn't over yet. If Tonya had Chloe, then she's got to be nearby."

Kate's eyes widened. "You think?"

"I do." He nodded to Angel. "If she is, Angel will track her." He hurried to the dog's side and untied her from the machine. "All right, Angel. Get the scent. Seek." He held the cloth to her, and she sniffed it then went into work mode. Her nose lifted in the air and she took off, heading for the woods.

THIRTEEN

Kate fell into step behind the two, her heart racing with hope once more. Angel seemed to get confused at one point, but after another sniff of the bib, her enthusiasm renewed, and she headed deeper into the trees. Kate stayed right behind them, holding Cocoa against her, pushing through the snow. Her legs ached, but she pressed on. She'd go for hours if it meant holding Chloe in her arms again.

Angel continued to pick her way through the trees until she came to a dirt path. A short distance later, Kate spotted a cabin in the distance in the middle of a large field. Smoke rose from the chimney, and there was a light in the far right window she assumed to be the kitchen. Angel lowered her nose to the ground then back up, trotted to the edge of the cabin and sat. Kate groaned. "She's lost it again?"

Despair welled, and she clenched her fists,

holding in the scream that wanted to escape. Instead, she planted her hands on her knees and pulled in a breath, trying to calm her racing heart and crashing hope.

Lucas tensed and called Angel back. He guided her and Kate behind a large stand of trees, then dropped to his knees to rub Angel's ears. "Good girl," he said. He slipped her a treat, and Angel gobbled it down.

Wait, what? "What do you mean, 'good girl'?"

"She sat," Lucas said. "It means this is where the scent runs out and, hopefully, we find Chloe."

Kate spun to look at the front door. "Inside there?"

He nodded, his eyes scanning the area. Kate tuned in, too. Part of her wanted to rush in and search the place, see if Chloe was in there. Another part of her wasn't sure she could handle the crushing disappointment if she discovered it was all just a false lead.

Lucas turned to her. "We know Tonya was working with a partner. Maybe her other son. Or just someone on the Maddox payroll. That guy could be in there. We have to be careful."

She nodded. Was Chloe in there with some criminal? She shivered.

Lucas checked his cell phone. "No signal." He dug his satellite phone from his pocket and called Tyson, reporting their location and updating him on the fact that they may have found Chloe. "I'll check back in with you in about half an hour." He hung up and nodded to Kate. "Ready?"

"Yes."

Angel tugged on the leash, and they darted behind the trees to the back of the cabin. Angel alerted again.

Kate stared up at the door to the cabin as a memory niggled at her.

"He's a nice guy. A real man's man," Nikki said with a short laugh. *"Spends a lot of time in his cabin in Sercy, Montana, hunting, fishing and doing all of those kinds of things."*

The conversation flooded her mind, and Kate shook her head.

"What is it?" Lucas asked.

"Just remembering. It's getting easier. And in remembering, I realized why I was so drawn to come out here."

"Why?"

"That one time Nikki mentioned Sean, she told me a little about him and that he came out to his cabin. In *Sercy,* Montana. And that he'd brought her here a few times. She said it was his and that he'd bought it with money not earned by his family." She grasped his forearm. "She told him she'd marry him, but only if he wasn't involved in his family's business." She blinked. "I have no idea why that memory just came to me, but…"

"I'm really glad you're remembering," he said. "Stay behind that tree," he said, unholstering his gun while he climbed the porch with Angel.

Lucas knocked. Silence echoed back at them.

He knocked again. "Rocky Mountain K-9 Unit. Open up!"

After a ten-second wait, Lucas turned the knob and pushed the door open. He held up his hand for Kate to stay where she was with Cocoa. The door gave a gentle bounce off the wall. "Hello?" From her vantage point, she could see through the opening. There was a great room and the kitchen just beyond. The table in the dining area held six chairs. And a high chair. The fire was still burning bright, like someone had just added a log.

"Someone's here," he whispered.

Movement to his left captured her attention. She got a glimpse of a man holding a gun, and there was no way Lucas could see him from his position. "He has a gun!"

Lucas turned and the man swung. His weapon connected with Lucas's skull with a sickening thud, and Lucas went to his knees.

Kate screamed, ran up the porch steps and launched herself at the attacker, but with Cocoa still in the pocket of the parka, she didn't dare grab him. Her hands landed on his chest, and her forward momentum knocked him off balance, but he quickly regained his balance and shrugged her off. She placed protective hands around Cocoa and landed on the floor with a painful thud. But her distraction was enough to allow Lucas to grab his gun and aim it at the man. "Get away from her!"

Angel went into a barking frenzy, which set off Cocoa. The man rolled and jammed his gun against Kate's temple. Everyone froze except the animals, whose ear-piercing barks echoed through the cabin.

"Shut them up!" the man said. "Now!"

"Angel, heel!" Angel darted to Lucas's side and Kate placed her hands around Cocoa, who fell quiet. Angel dropped beside Lucas, who still held his weapon on the man holding Kate.

Kate stayed still, not daring to move.

"Drop it," he said. "Or she dies."

The pressure on her head increased, and

she winced. Lucas held her gaze, the torment there reaching deep within her. "No," she mouthed. "Don't."

But he lowered the weapon to the floor then held his hands up in the universal gesture of surrender.

"Kick it over here and keep your hands where I can see them."

"You're David Maddox," Lucas said, and Kate knew he was trying to buy time. "Tonya's son."

The man ignored that. "Do what I tell you!"

Lucas did as ordered, and Kate's hope deflated like a pierced balloon, but at least the weapon fell from her head. He gave her a rough shove toward Lucas then bent to snag the gun from the floor. Once the man had both weapons, he backed up, keeping them covered with his gun.

She knelt beside Lucas to check his head. He looked dazed and slightly sick. And as mad as a teased hornet. "You okay?" she asked.

"Yeah."

"I'm sorry," she whispered.

Kate kept her eyes on the man with the guns. He reached into his pocket, pulled out a zip tie and tossed it to Kate. "Put his hands behind his back and make sure he can't get out of that. I'm going to check it, so make sure it's right."

With shaky fingers, Kate grabbed the tie and looked at Lucas. With his hands behind his back...

"Just do it," he said, "You have no choice."

She did the job but left it looser than their captor would probably like. She'd let him tighten it if he wanted. "There." Now she had to figure out how to help him get out of it.

David waved the gun at her. "Get in the chair over there. In the corner."

Kate walked to the chair and sat. From her vantage point, she had a view of the whole room, including the kitchen. The bay window was to her left. To her right, Lucas was seated on the floor next to the front door with Angel at his side, her body bristling at the tension coming off her handler. Cocoa whined and wiggled to get out of her cocoon. "May I let her out?" Kate asked.

"What?"

"The dog." She pointed to her parka pocket. "Can I let her out? She wants to be with Angel. I have her on a leash so I can tie her to the chair next to Lucas."

For a moment, the man looked confused, like he wasn't sure whether he should allow it or not. Then he nodded. She removed Cocoa from the front pocket and did as she'd suggested. Cocoa was happy and curled next to her friend. With Cocoa settled, that left Kate's hands free in case she needed them for whatever reason. Like to fight back—or grab a weapon.

The man checked her work with a glance from a safe distance. He wasn't giving Lucas any opportunity to make a move against him, and Kate wished she'd left the tie even looser.

Shoving aside her regrets, she studied their captor. He still looked familiar—and she *still* didn't know why. "Why are you doing this? Where's Chloe?"

"How did you find this place?" Maddox countered.

"Angel—the dog—found it."

"How!"

She glanced at Lucas, and he nodded, giving her the okay to tell this man only what he needed to know to not become infuriated. That she knew Lucas so well was unsettling.

Holding on to her fear by a thread, wondering what to say, but mostly what *not* to say, Kate held up the pink bib. "Someone tried to kill us by shooting up the cabin where we were staying, and we—ah—found this. Angel is a tracking dog. She led us to this place."

He stared at the piece of cloth, brows forming a fierce V over the bridge of his nose. "Where's my mother?"

Kate could see the family resemblance to Sean Maddox. She'd only seen his picture one time, but that had been all she needed for her artistic brain to imprint it in her memory. She was quite sure Sean was Chloe's father, but she needed this monster to confirm it. "Who is Chloe to you?" she asked, her voice low, avoiding his question for now.

"She's my niece, and she belongs to the Maddox family according to my mother."

"You look very much like your brother. Close enough to be mistaken for twins. Which is why I recognized you outside the sheriff's office."

"Impressive. You got it on the first try." He snorted. "Sean and I were only fifteen months apart. And yeah, we looked alike." He cursed. "I knew you'd remember. That stupid shrink said you probably wouldn't."

Kate gasped. "My *shrink*? Bryan Gold talked to you?"

"How do you think we managed to find you and stay updated on everything? Including the fact that your memory was returning. He was very eager to help as long as the money was flowing."

Kate's mouth worked as she tried to process the betrayal. "But this time, he didn't know where I was. Pretty smart of you to put the tracker on the sheriff's car."

Lucas glared at the guy. "That whole thing in the parking lot at the sheriff's office. You planned to put a tracker on *my* SUV, didn't you?"

It was the only explanation.

David raised a brow. "Yeah, that was the original plan, but I was afraid someone would find it after all the attention I wound up getting. Since you'd had an escort before, I figured the sheriff would probably do it again." He frowned. "I was trying to be more subtle about it than it all went down, but I hit a little patch of ice and nearly slammed into the vehicle."

Kate replayed the moment in her head, seeing his handlebars jerk and how he'd disappeared behind the vehicle.

"Made it a little harder to find you, but once I realized you were going up the mountain, it didn't take too much time to find your vehicle."

Just like they'd thought.

"So, you got the tracker on the sheriff's cruiser," she said. "You came to do what you'd intended. Why did you try to open the doors to Lucas's car?"

"To let the dogs out. Figured I'd send them running, and you'd be too busy chasing them to worry about the guy who crashed the bike." His jaw hardened. "Of course, you had to be looking out the window and see everything."

"It was you the whole time?" she whispered. "You and your mother working together? With my therapist?" Nausea had a firm grip on her throat, and she swallowed hard. "I don't believe this." She raked a hand over her head and pulled the hat off. "Was that you in my bedroom that night?"

He rubbed his hand and scowled. "Yeah. I owe you for that one. Can't believe you stabbed me. Who keeps a knife on their nightstand?"

"It was a letter opener," she muttered, then shuddered and moved on to her next question while he appeared not to mind them—and to pull his focus away from the fact she'd stabbed him. "And on the road after Lucas picked me up? Who was that? Tonya?"

"Yes. When I called and filled her in, she took over. Rode out to the entrance to the subdivision and just waited for you to leave. Followed you until she thought she had a good chance to run you off the road."

"But that didn't work," Lucas said.

"Nope." He scratched his chin. "She was flaming mad. Figured you'd have contact with the sheriff at some point so told me to go watch and wait." He snorted. "Took you long enough to come to town."

Where he'd been ready with a plan to get that tracker on whatever vehicle they used. Then adjusted the plan when he had to.

"Where's Chloe?" Lucas demanded.

"She's around."

"Where?"

"Close by. Now shut up."

'Close by'? She couldn't stop the surge of hope, but…what did 'close by' actually mean? "What happens now?" she asked.

He sighed as though she was trying his patience. "My mother will make that call. She's the one in charge. She should be here any minute now."

Did he not know that the woman had planned to kill them at the cabin? "Your mother is—" She bit off the word "dead" and shot a glance at Lucas. If he knew the woman had died, what would he do?

"Where is she?" Lucas asked, sliding a glance at her. He clearly didn't want David to know his mother was dead. Maddox's fury could get them both killed.

"On an errand," David said. "She said she was going to take care of something, and I was to keep an eye on—" He clamped his lips together. "Anyway, when she gets back, she'll tell me what the plan is. Until then, we'll just sit tight."

But the woman wasn't coming back. What would happen once he realized that?

A baby's cry sounded from down the hall, and Kate froze. Her gaze jerked to Lucas's and his eyes widened.

"Chloe," Kate whispered. Well, David hadn't lied. The baby was definitely close by. With everything in her, she wanted to run toward the sound, but did she dare?

David jerked the gun at her. "Go get the kid and shut her up."

Kate hurried down the hall to the back bedroom. She stepped inside to see Chloe standing in a beautiful ornate crib, her tiny hands clasping the rail. When she saw Kate, her eyes widened and her cries stopped. Kate walked to the crib and picked up the baby, taking in the familiar features. She'd missed the last eight months of Chloe's life, but she would have recognized the child anywhere. She had the same striking blue eyes and while her cry had matured, she still sounded pretty much the same. "Oh, Chloe." Chloe stuck a finger in her mouth and frowned at her, like she thought she should know the woman holding her but wasn't sure she recognized her. Then decided she didn't care and wailed once more. "Shh, baby," Kate whispered, "it's okay." She looked around the room, desperately searching for something she could use as a weapon.

"What are you doing?" David called. "Get back in here!"

"I'm…changing her." She did need a diaper. Kate found the stack, along with a carton of wipes, on the changing table next to the crib.

"Oh. Well, hurry up!"

"I'm hurrying." She changed the baby at lightning speed. That seemed to solve the most immediate issue as Chloe stopped fussing, but she never took her eyes off Kate's face. Kate picked her up, relishing the fact that she had the child in her arms once more, and hurried to the bathroom.

Baby stuff was scattered everywhere.

"What's taking so long?"

Kate's heart pounded, but she couldn't leave without—

There.

Baby nail clippers. They'd have to do. She grabbed them from the little grooming set, opened them and curled them into her palm. "Coming!"

She walked down the hall and back into the den, where she found Lucas still but more clear-eyed in spite of the fact that the wound on his head had to be pounding. He raised a brow at her, the movement subtle, but the meaning clear. Was she okay? She nodded and stopped, turning her body slightly to keep the gun on her, not Chloe. "Can I show him the baby?" she asked.

David blinked. "What?"

"He's been searching for her for the past eight months. I just want him to see her." Did it sound suspicious? Like a flimsy excuse to get close to Lucas? "Please?"

"Whatever." He motioned with the weapon, signaling her to show the baby to Lucas, and she moved close. She dropped to her knees next to him and he frowned, obviously realizing she was up to something but unsure of his role in it.

"Look at her, Lucas," she said. "Isn't she perfect?"

"Absolutely."

Kate held Chloe with her right arm around the child's midsection and moved her left around to his hands tied at his back. She nudged one and it fell open. "I wish you could hold her, but you finally found her. You and Angel."

At her name, the dog's ears twitched and she gazed at Kate.

Kate dropped the clippers into Lucas's hand, and he curled his fingers around them.

"All right, all right," David said, "that's enough. I don't know what's taking my mother so long. Get over there in the chair and sit down. I'm going to call her and see what I need to do." He grabbed the satellite phone from the end table and dialed.

Lucas stiffened at the man's mention of his mother but was busy trying to maneuver the opened clippers around so he could snip at the zip tie. The cabin was warm, and he was hot in his heavy coat.

His eyes stayed on Kate. She lowered herself into the chair as ordered, but he could tell she was ready to act the moment he gave her a signal.

"My mother isn't answering," David muttered, letting out a frustrated cry and slammed the phone on the table by the recliner opposite Kate. She jumped and pulled Chloe a little closer.

"How did you know Sean was Chloe's father?" Lucas asked. "From what I understand, Nikki wasn't exactly advertising the fact. According to our investigation, everything points to the fact that she was desperately trying to hide it."

"Sean was furious when Nikki broke it off with him." David smirked. "I think my brother was actually in love for the first time in his life. He told our mother that he was done with the family business—"

"The business of killing people?" Kate muttered.

"—and that he was going to settle down," he said as though Kate hadn't spoken, "marry this Nikki girl and go straight. He was going to cut all ties with us. He was even working a legitimate job with some construction company."

Kate blinked, and Lucas wondered if she was remembering this as something Nikki had told her or if it was all new to her.

"Mom was furious. She put a tail on Sean.

She had to know who this woman was. When the guy came back and reported that Sean's girlfriend was pregnant, things got real heated."

"Let me guess," Lucas said. "It wasn't too long after that when Sean was killed in a car accident."

His scowl deepened. "A week later. Why?"

"Just starting to put it all together."

David lifted the weapon and pointed it at Lucas. "You trying to say she had something to do with Sean's death?"

Lucas held his gaze. "I'm not saying anything of the sort. As far as I remember, it was ruled an accident. Rainy night, slippery road."

"Exactly." The gun lowered a fraction, and Lucas scrambled to keep him talking while another part of his brain worked on a plan. It might take sheer muscle to get out of this one. The guy was small, but Lucas's head beat a painful rhythm while nausea continued to taunt him.

Lucas swallowed. "What I'm saying is I don't think it's a stretch to think that that's when she started planning to kidnap Chloe once she was born."

Lucas sucked in another breath and got the clippers situated once more around the plastic.

Chloe let out a cry and jammed her fist into her mouth. Kate looked at their captor. "She's hungry."

"And my mother will feed her when she gets here."

Kate's eyes blazed, but she bit her lip. "I understand that you want to wait on her, but if you know anything about babies, you know they're not very patient. Can you handle her fussing until your mom gets here to feed her?"

As if on cue, Chloe let out another wail.

"No!" David raked a hand over his head, and the weapon shook. "Just…feed her. Do whatever you have to do to keep her quiet. There are bottles and that formula stuff in the kitchen. I think there are some jars of baby food, too. I don't know what all she needs."

Kate nodded. "Well, I do. I can take care of her if you'll let me."

"Yeah, yeah. Fine."

With another look at Lucas, Kate rose and carried Chloe into the kitchen.

Lucas needed a plan, but so far he hadn't managed to come up with one. His cell phone was still on the clip on his belt. The man had seen it but hadn't bothered to tell him to get rid of it, so he could only assume he wasn't worried about it because there wasn't a signal.

The satellite phone on the end table next to the recliner was also a good indication of that. "What is taking her so long?" David muttered. He walked to the device and picked it up. But the gun in his hand never lowered.

Lucas cleared his throat. "What's the plan here, man? Your mother kidnapped a baby and killed a woman—the baby's mother. She's tried to kill Kate several times." He hesitated. "You're not in the system yet. Are you sure you want to go down with her?"

David raised a brow at him. "I'm not in the system? How do you know?"

"DNA testing." He shot a pointed look at the man's shoulder. "You left some behind."

"Oh." He scowled.

"You said your mother calls the shots. Do you do everything she says?"

"If I want to keep breathing, I do."

Lucas finally wedged the zip tie between the blades of the small clippers. He gently squeezed and felt them cut through the plastic. Silently, he applauded Kate, whose gaze bounced between the two of them while she held Chloe.

The satellite phone rang, and David grabbed it. "Where are you?" A pause. "Oh. I thought you were my mother. No, I haven't heard from her." Lucas tensed. Once he knew his mother was dead, things could go south quickly. "Uh-huh," David said. "Well, find her and tell her to call me. I have a situation I need her help with." He listened. "It doesn't matter what kind of situation. Just tell her to call me!" He hung up and slammed the phone back onto the table.

"Problem?" Lucas asked. He wondered who that was—Bryan Gold?

"Yeah, but it's mine and not yours."

"So, we just sit here until your mother comes back?"

"Yes. Now, shut up so I can think."

Lucas fell silent and worked the clippers for another cut. The zip tie fell from his wrists, and he flexed them, feeling hope rise that they might get out of this alive after all. The satellite phone in his pocket could be easily traced by Tyson or any member of the unit. They just had to realize he needed help. Hopefully, they could stay alive long enough for Tyson to realize they were in trouble.

FOURTEEN

Kate couldn't stop herself from watching the clock. The more the minutes ticked past, the more her stomach twisted into knots. David had started to pace exactly three minutes ago.

Lucas kept his hands behind him, and she couldn't tell if he'd managed to get out of the zip tie or not.

David made a pass into the kitchen and opened the refrigerator. She flexed her hands around the baby, who had finished about half the bottle. David seemed willing enough to let her care for Chloe, but he certainly didn't trust her, and she'd noticed he was careful to watch her.

But not so careful about keeping an eye on Lucas. She let her gaze meet Lucas's, and he shot her a tight smile. He looked at Chloe then at the hall. Back to the baby, then the hall again.

Okay, he was trying to tell her something. When David's back was turned once more, she pointed to herself, Chloe and then the hall with a raised brow.

He nodded.

She cleared her throat. "Um, David?"

He raised his head and glared at her from his stance in front of the refrigerator. "What?"

"I need to change Chloe again."

"Again? Seriously?"

"She's a baby." Kate left it at that.

He waved a hand toward the room at the end of the hall. "You know where the stuff is." He had the satellite phone once more and punched in a number.

Kate met Lucas's eyes once more, and he nodded to the hall. Kate didn't know what he was planning, but something was up and he wanted her and Chloe out of the way. Keeping Chloe safe was the priority, of course, but she wasn't letting Lucas do something alone. She placed Chloe in the crib with her stuffed bunny and her bottle.

But first, they had to get away from the man in the den. A low rumble reached her, and she listened for a second before identifying the sound as a helicopter in the distance.

With Chloe happily distracted at the moment, Kate walked back down the hall making eye contact with David, who still paced. He stopped and she did, too. "Where is she?" he asked.

Kate frowned. "I put her in her crib."

"Not her! My mother! She always answers her phone, and she wouldn't leave the kid with me for this long. She's obsessed with her. All because she's Sean's." The flicker of jealousy was clear. "Ah, my head. All of this is giving me a migraine just thinking about it. Where's my mother!" He placed both hands against his temples, the gun pointed upward.

Like a flash, Lucas moved and slammed into the man. They crashed into the bay window. Glass shattered, and they fell out onto the snow. Angel barked and followed, lunging toward the man threatening her handler. Kate bit down on a scream and raced to the window.

Chopper blades beat the air above, and a spotlight swept the area.

Lucas had his hand wrapped around David's wrist. Heart pounding, Kate stepped on the windowsill and pushed herself through to the ground. To her horror, in spite of his smaller stature, David seemed to be getting the upper hand—probably thanks to the head wound slowing Lucas down.

She spun back to the broken window, grabbed the lamp from the end table and whirled back to see David had rolled on top. She bolted to the two men just as Angel latched on to David's ankle. He screamed and froze, and in that split second, she brought the lamp down on his head.

He went limp, and the gun fell into the snow.

Breathing hard, Lucas rolled out from under from the man and looked up at her. "Thank you." He fished for the gun in the snow, found it and shoved it into his pocket.

Kate dropped beside him and cupped his face. "Are you all right?"

"Thanks to you."

The chopper landed in the open area fifty yards away, and a uniformed officer and his dog exited the belly followed by others.

"All clear!" Lucas shouted out to the officer. "That's my new colleague, Gavin Walker and his K-9, Koda." A few other RMKU members leaped out with their K-9s.

"How'd they find us?" Kate asked.

"Tyson probably sent them when I didn't check in like I told him I would. And when I didn't answer my cell or the satellite phone, he probably figured I needed reinforcements."

While Gavin and Koda made their way toward them, the others rushed toward David Maddox. Lucas scooted next to David and felt for a pulse. He looked up at her. "He's alive."

Her shoulders wilted. She would have done whatever it took to keep Lucas safe, but she was glad she hadn't had to kill to do it. Then she gasped. "Angel! She jumped through the window. The glass…"

"She has her boots on. She's fine." He turned to Kate and pulled her into a tight hug. "She's fine. We're fine. Chloe's fine."

"It's finally over," she whispered. "Thank you."

"Don't thank me. It was all Angel. When she bit David's ankle, it gave you the time to hit him."

At the sound of her name, the border collie bounded over while Cocoa barked her displeasure at being left tied up in the cabin. The officers cuffed the unconscious man and carted him toward the chopper.

Gavin approached, and after Lucas's introduction, Kate pulled from his grasp. "I'm going to get Chloe."

"Yeah. I'll be right behind you," Lucas said. "I just need to tell Gavin to call Tyson and Skylar and let them know to go after Bryan Gold."

Kate shook her head at what her therapist had been a part of, but her mind was on Chloe and having the baby safely in her arms.

She headed for the front door, her heart pounding hard enough to feel it in her head. She heard Lucas tell Gavin to make the call about Bryan Gold, then he followed her into the cabin, all the way down the hall, to find Chloe had fallen asleep, but she stirred at their entrance. Kate walked over to the crib and gathered the baby into her arms. Finally. Tears clogged her throat, and she kissed the sweet little head. "I've got you, Chloe. You're safe, and I'm going to make sure you stay that way the rest of your life. Forever. I promise."

Lucas moved in closer, and she looked up at him. "Can I get in on this?"

Kate bit her lip at the look in his eyes. "You're sure?"

He nodded. "As sure as I was when I decided to become a K-9 handler."

She smiled. "That's pretty sure. I didn't think you were up for risking your heart again after…everything."

He reached up and grasped her biceps, pulling her close so he could press a kiss to

her forehead. Then one to Chloe's cheek.
When he lifted his head, he locked his gaze
with hers once more. "I came to realize something."

"What's that?"

"I was looking at relationships all wrong.
I kept thinking of a relationship as taking a
calculated risk—and deciding whether it was
worth it or not. But since meeting you, I realized I wasn't doing that with you. I can't
explain how it happened over the last few
weeks, but I don't consider you—us—a 'risk.'
I believe we're a sure thing. The right thing
and... I've fallen in love with you, Kate."

Kate's breath caught in her throat.

"You don't have to—"

She placed a finger against his lips. "I feel
the same way, Lucas. I do. And I believe with
all my heart we're a sure thing, but I come as
a package. Are you sure—"

"I'm sure. We've been looking for Chloe
for so long—and to be a part of finding her—
well, I feel like she already belongs to me in
a way. Being able to love her and watch her
grow up with you is the best thing I could
ever dream of. Can we see where all of this
will take us? Can we plan and dream and
build a life together?"

"Absolutely."

His eyes lit up, and he leaned in to settle his lips over hers. The warmth his kiss generated went all the way to her toes, and she leaned in, head swimming from sheer relief and the fact that she could finally allow herself to recognize the feelings of love that had been building since the first moment she'd laid eyes on Lucas. When he lifted his head, she snuggled against him while Chloe giggled and patted his cheek.

With joy soaring, she leaned back to grin up at him. "Definitely a sure thing."

EPILOGUE

With Angel trotting at his side, Lucas walked into the RMKU headquarters, glad to be back in Denver, but knowing that little duplex cabin in Montana would always hold a special place in his heart.

Kate and Chloe would be meeting him here shortly, and they would all ride together to New Mexico to cheer on his former RMKU team member Daniella Vargas and her fiancé, Sam Kavanagh, as they promised to spend the rest of their lives together in wedded bliss.

Lucas smiled. Wedded bliss was a myth. No one knew that more so than he, but after seeing all of the weddings and happiness his team had found, it confirmed what he'd believed all along. Marriage could definitely be a good thing when both parties were fully committed—in the good times and the bad. Something he was ready to take a chance on with the one person that could make him break a promise to himself. Kate Montgomery had his heart and taking it back wasn't an option. So, he planned to see her as often as possible, and if things kept going the way they did since they'd gone on the run together, then he planned to ask her to marry him.

If she'd have him.

His heart pounded at the thought, but he was quite sure she would. Sure enough that he'd already bought the ring.

Because they were a sure thing.

But first things first. He walked into the conference room to find the entire team gathered and waiting for his report. They chatted and caught up with one another while the dogs lounged under the chairs, enjoying the respite and relaxed atmosphere. "Hey, everyone, Kate and Chloe will be here any second so we can get on the road to Sam and Daniella's wedding." Cheers went up and he grinned. "I can see I'm going to have to keep this short." More clapping ensued and he laughed with them only to be distracted when, through the open conference room door, he saw Kate walking down the hall with a pink-dressed Chloe in her arms. He waved for her to join them and set his notes on the podium. He didn't really need them.

Kate stepped inside, and everyone smiled at the sight. The fact that Kate was alive and had been reunited with Chloe was a forceful reminder of why they did what they did. Kate and Chloe were one of their biggest success stories, and the emotion on each face made his own throat tighten. He cleared it. "Kate, you and Chloe can take a seat in the chair up here next to me." He patted the cushion, and Kate walked the length of the room to sit beside him. Chloe looked up at him and grinned. He tapped her nose and the baby chuckled. She was a happy child in spite of her tumultuous first year.

"All right, everyone. Most of you know the details of everything that went down, but here's the official version. Tonya Maddox and her son David Maddox were the ones who caused the wreck that almost killed Kate..." Just saying the words sent his fingers curling into fists at his sides. He took a deep breath. "They're also the ones who kidnapped Chloe and bribed Kate's therapist, Bryan Gold, to keep them updated on her whereabouts and progress remembering that night. Once Tonya Maddox learned Nikki Baker was pregnant with Sean's child, she determined that the baby would be raised by the family."

"And was willing to kill to make that happen," Tyson said.

"Yes."

The others nodded.

"And as far as Bryan Gold is concerned, he's been arrested and is in police custody, stripped of his license and begging the DA for a deal."

"It's a shame," Kate said, her voice soft. "Seems like people will do anything for money."

"Bryan was struggling financially," Lucas said. "He'd made some really bad investment choices. He was getting ready to lose his wife, his house, his business. Everything."

"And now he's lost that *and* his freedom."

Chloe chose that moment to squeal and wiggled, kicking to get down, while reaching for Angel. Kate set her on the floor next to the dog. Angel swiped Chloe's cheek with her tongue, making Chloe laugh. Lucas grinned. "But enough about business. We have a wedding to get to. Chloe, want me to carry you?"

Chloe used Angel's back to pull herself to her feet, and Kate gasped when the little girl let go and stood there. "Lucas, look."

"I see." He walked to kneel two feet from Chloe and held his hands out. "Come here, Chloe. Walk to me. You can do it."

After a brief hesitation, she took three steps before she wobbled and Lucas caught her. Clapping erupted, and Chloe looked startled for a moment then grinned and clapped, too. Lucas found Kate watching with a huge smile on her face. "Those were her very first steps."

Lucas smiled, unable to stop his throat going tight with all of the emotions swirling through him. He was so blessed. So very blessed.

He cleared his throat. "Everyone ready to party?"

Tyson stood. "Count me in. All right, everyone," he said. "Time to roll. We've got a wedding to get to. The lobby is full of impatient spouses, fiancés and whatnot." Everyone laughed. "Let's not keep them waiting."

Lucas waited until everyone was out of the room then walked over to Kate. "You ready?"

"I am, but I have something to tell you first."

"What?" He shifted Chloe to his other hip.

"My father called me just a little while ago."

Lucas hoped he was able to maintain an innocent expression. "Really?"

Kate gave his bicep a light punch. "Nice try. He said you called him."

A flush crept up his neck. "Oh. He wasn't supposed to tell you that part."

"Well, he did." Her eyes reddened and tears formed for a brief second.

"Oh no. Did I really mess it up?"

"No." She sniffed. "He said you set him straight. And that he was going to talk some sense into my mother."

"Oh good." Relief weakened his knees, and he locked them. "But I suppose I owe you an apology if I overstepped."

"No, it's okay. They want to meet when we get back from the wedding and—"

Again, the tears appeared.

"What is it, Kate?"

"He said he wants to come to my show in New York," she whispered. This time two tears managed to escape and trailed down her cheeks.

He used his thumb to swipe them away. "Please tell me those are happy tears."

"Yes." She sniffed and laughed. "They're happy tears."

"Then I'm happy, too."

"I've dreamed of this, Lucas. I mean literally dreamed of having them express an interest in my art. I never imagined they'd actually come to a show, but..."

"They are," he finished for her.

She nodded.

He cleared his throat. "I…ah…have something I want to ask you."

Her eyes widened, and she nodded. "Okay."

Still holding Chloe, he pulled out the ring he'd slipped into his pocket. "I hope now is okay to ask this, but I honestly don't think I can wait another minute. But I also don't want to hijack Sam and Daniella's day."

"Oh, Lucas…"

"I want to spend the rest of my life with you and Chloe." He held the ring up. "Will you and Chloe marry me?"

She sucked in a breath, met his gaze and nodded. "Yes."

He slid the ring on her shaking hand and pulled her closer for a long kiss.

"Hey," Tyson said, poking his head back into the room, "not to interrupt, but are you three coming?"

"We are," Lucas said. "Just clearing some things up."

"Right. Well, come on."

He ducked out, and Lucas shook his head. "I guess we'd better go."

She nodded. "I guess so."

He leaned over to kiss her again. "I love you, Kate."

"I love you, too, Lucas."

"And, I'll admit, I love this kiddo here like I wouldn't have thought possible."

She smiled. "I know. She knows it, too." She nodded to Chloe who'd laid her head on Lucas's shoulder. Kate looped her arm through his free elbow and aimed them toward the door. "Come on, Mr. Sure Thing. You heard the man. It's time to get to a wedding."

"Yeah. This one. Next one's ours, deal?"

"Deal."

* * * * *

Don't miss two bonus Christmas novellas in, Christmas K-9 Heroes, and the rest of the Rocky Mountain K-9 Unit series:

Dear Reader,

Thank you so much for coming along on the Rocky Mountain K-9 Unit adventure. I had the honor of writing book 8 and wrapping up baby Chloe's story. I also loved writing about Angel, the Search and Rescue dog, and Cocoa, the emotional support animal. Dogs are such amazing creatures. The unconditional love that they lavish on us is so undeserved, but so rewarding to be the recipient of that love. And Lucas and Kate were such fabulous characters to create and make come to life. They had a rough start, but thankfully, all worked out for them and they got their happily ever after. I pray that you were able to lose yourself in this book and escape your trouble for a few hours. Thank you again, for reading. And I hope you'll keep looking for the next K-9 continuity series. I know you won't want to miss it.

God Bless,
Lynette

Get 4 FREE REWARDS!

We'll send you 2 FREE Books plus 2 FREE Mystery Gifts.

FREE Value Over $20

Both the **Love Inspired®** and **Love Inspired®** Suspense series feature compelling novels filled with inspirational romance, faith, forgiveness, and hope.

YES! Please send me 2 FREE novels from the Love Inspired or Love Inspired Suspense series and my 2 FREE gifts (gifts are worth about $10 retail). After receiving them, if I don't wish to receive any more books, I can return the shipping statement marked "cancel." If I don't cancel, I will receive 6 brand-new Love Inspired Larger-Print books or Love Inspired Suspense Larger-Print books every month and be billed just $6.24 each in the U.S. or $6.49 each in Canada. That is a savings of at least 17% off the cover price. It's quite a bargain! Shipping and handling is just 50¢ per book in the U.S. and $1.25 per book in Canada.* I understand that accepting the 2 free books and gifts places me under no obligation to buy anything. I can always return a shipment and cancel at any time by calling the number below. The free books and gifts are mine to keep no matter what I decide.

Choose one: ☐ **Love Inspired**   ☐ **Love Inspired Suspense**
Larger-Print   Larger-Print
(122/322 IDN GRDF)   (107/307 IDN GRDF)

Name (please print)

Address   Apt. #

City   State/Province   Zip/Postal Code

Email: Please check this box ☐ if you would like to receive newsletters and promotional emails from Harlequin Enterprises ULC and its affiliates. You can unsubscribe anytime.

Mail to the **Harlequin Reader Service:**
IN U.S.A.: P.O. Box 1341, Buffalo, NY 14240-8531
IN CANADA: P.O. Box 603, Fort Erie, Ontario L2A 5X3

Want to try 2 free books from another series! Call 1-800-873-8635 or visit www.ReaderService.com.